New Girl in Town

Cedar River Daydreams

Other Books by Judy Baer

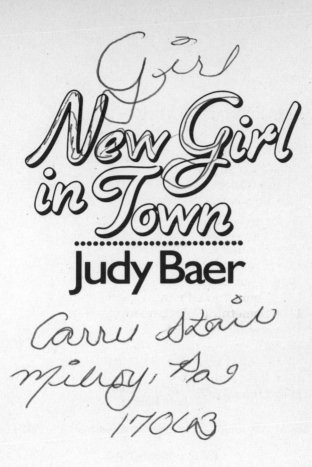

New Girl in Town

Judy Baer

Carri Stail
milloy, Pa
17063

BETHANY HOUSE PUBLISHERS
MINNEAPOLIS, MINNESOTA 55438

New Girl in Town
Judy Baer

Library of Congress Catalog Card Number 88–71504

ISBN 1-55661-022-X

Published by Bethany House Publishers
A Ministry of Bethany Fellowship, Inc.
6820 Auto Club Road, Minneapolis, Minnesota 55438

Printed in the United States of America

This series is dedicated to my daughters,
Adrienne and Jennifer Baer,
with a love that no writer or words
can adequately express.

JUDY BAER received a B.A. in English and Education from Concordia College in Moorhead, Minnesota. She has had ten novels published and is a member of the National Romance Writers of America, the Society of Children's Book Writers and the National Federation of Press Women.

Two of her novels have been prizewinning bestsellers in the Bethany House SPRINGFLOWER SERIES (for girls 12–15); *Adrienne* and *Paige*. Both books have been awarded first place for juvenile fiction in the National Federation of Press Women's communications contest.

Chapter One

"I wish we'd never come. Never."

"Now, Alexis. You'll get used to Cedar River and then you'll wonder why you ever thought you didn't like it here. Give yourself some time." Mrs. Leighton skimmed her fingers through her daughter's thick blond hair. "Patience, honey."

"I've been patient," Lexi groaned. "I've been patient for days, but nothing has happened. I've hardly met a soul. If I were home right now, the phone would be ringing and . . ." Her brown eyes flickered with dismay.

"You *are* home. This is your *new* home."

"Well, I wish it weren't." Lexi slipped off the kitchen stool and began to pace around the sunlit room. "I was popular in my old school. I had lots of friends and we had things to do every day. Here I'm just a—a nobody!"

It wasn't easy starting over at sixteen in a new city where no one knew her—or cared if they ever did. At home she'd had all the friends she'd ever wanted. Here, in Cedar River, it seemed there wasn't a single person interested in finding out who Lexi Leighton was.

Mrs. Leighton smiled. "You're the prettiest nobody I've ever seen—and the most vocal. Just be who you are, Lexi, and people won't be able to resist."

Lexi registered a doubtful scowl. Every word Mrs. Leighton said was mother-talk. It was meant to make her feel better—like soft tissues and chicken soup when she had a cold. But Lexi was suffering far worse than she ever had from any cold. Moving was like . . . major illness.

It had been important to her father to come to Cedar River. It was his opportunity to open his own veterinary clinic in a city that needed an animal clinic for exotic and domestic pets.

"I'll bet Cory and Denise are going to the pool right now," she sighed. "I'd already be there lifeguarding with the rest of the gang. After the pool closed we'd practice diving for a while and then all dry off and head to our house for—"

"I realize it's been quiet, Lexi. I know that our house was the stopping-off point for every student in the sophomore and junior classes, but things will improve here—wait and see."

Usually she believed her mom, but not this time. Cedar River was a city, not a little drop-in-the-bucket town like Grover's Point. Here, who'd even care that she existed?

The telephone rang near her ear. Out of habit, Lexi lunged for it. Then as she cradled it in her palm, she remembered, *But it can't be for me. It never is.*

"Hullo, Leightons'? Is Lexi there?"

"Speaking." Her heartbeat speeded up a bit.

"This is Jennifer Golden. We met at the musical. I'm going to rehearsal now. Want to walk with me?"

"Sure. Great! I'll meet you out front."

"Okay. Bye."

Lexi could hear Jennifer snapping her gum as she hung up.

Mrs. Leighton was grinning. "I told you things would work out. Already someone is calling you."

"Jennifer and I aren't much alike, Mom."

"Since when did that bother you? You never worried about having friends who were like you before." Mrs. Leighton chuckled. "I doubt that another person exists who even *faintly* resembles you. Anyway, you brought home some very odd people who turned out to be awfully nice. Don't change now!"

Lexi grinned in spite of herself. Her mother was referring to Lexi's passion for wearing the crazy clothes she herself designed and sewed and for the assorted collection of friends she'd enjoyed. It was true that she'd marched to the beat of her own drummer, no matter what others thought, and it had always worked out. Even the move had sounded exciting when her father first brought it up.

But now that they were living in Cedar River, the excitement had been replaced by misery. Lexi had never felt so alone in her entire life.

"Jennifer's meeting me out front. We're going to practice for the summer musical. See you!" Lexi ducked out of the house before her mother could assure her again that everything would work out. That was especially hard to listen to when she was unconvinced that things would ever be fine again.

"Hi, Lexi!" her little brother called from the porch swing.

"Hi, Ben."

"Play?"

"Can't play right now. I've got rehearsal to go to." Her step slowed. "But I will when I get back."

"Please?"

"Later, honey. See? There's Jennifer coming down the street. She'll be waiting for me."

"Please?"

Lexi took time to plant a kiss on the top of Ben's silky brown head before she turned to run down the steps. She moved through the gate and onto the sidewalk to match steps with Jennifer. Halfway down the block, she turned to glance over her shoulder.

Ben was crying. Lexi stared at him, sadness and a tinge of anger in her dark eyes.

He can't ruin things for me. Not now, she petitioned silently. But the damage had already been done.

"What's wrong with your brother, Lexi? Is he hurt?" Jennifer inquired.

Lexi's one and only acquaintance in Cedar River slowed her stride and peered through long blond bangs at the small boy whimpering and clinging to the closed gate through which they had just passed. Jennifer, tall and athletic looking with the most incredibly large and beautiful blue eyes, stared curiously at Ben. He made a pitiful sight swinging forlornly on the Leightons' gate.

"No. He just wants to come along. Since we moved here he's spent most of his days with me. He can't understand why I'm leaving him behind."

"Heavy." Jennifer snapped the double wad of gum in her mouth and stared back at Ben.

A wave of irritation swept over Lexi. Oh, how she missed her old friends!

"I don't know how you can take it, Lexi. I couldn't stand having a squalling brat around me all the time." Jennifer cracked her gum in exclamation. "What's wrong with him, anyway?"

"I told you. He's just lonesome. I've been with him every day for two weeks and now he doesn't want me to leave."

"No. I mean *really* wrong with him? How come he looks so different from you? And he sure doesn't act like *my* brother did when he was eight!"

"Ben has Down's syndrome, Jennifer." Lexi's chin lifted as she spoke.

"What's *that*?" Jennifer stopped walking and made a one hundred and eighty degree turn on the sidewalk. She squinted as she looked back to the now small figure swinging on the Leightons' gate.

Lexi tugged at Jennifer's elbow. "Come on. We're going to be late for practice. I started rehearsal a week behind as it is. I can't afford to miss a minute."

"But what *is* Down's whatever? How come it makes him that way?"

Fingers of irritation snapped in Lexi's brain. At home—her old home—everyone had known about Ben. Now she'd have to start explaining all over again.

"Down's syndrome is a genetic imbalance caused by an extra set of chromosome genes. It happens when something goes wrong in the division of cells before a baby is born." She paused for a moment. "Ben's retarded."

Thinking about it made her angry—especially now—when just being in this new place seemed so difficult. Why *had* God allowed this to happen to Ben? she wondered. *Why?*

"So what will he be like, then? When he grows up, I mean?" Jennifer's eyes glinted with curiosity. She brushed her thick bangs to one side and stared at Lexi.

"Ben's very bright, considering his handicaps," Lexi murmured, trying not to sound defensive. "Someday he'll probably train for a job of some sort."

"Really? I thought people like that would never— well, you know!" Jennifer had the grace to look embarrassed.

Lexi bit her lower lip. People had a lot to learn about kids like Ben.

"Have your parents ever thought of putting him in an institution?" Jennifer inquired.

"The doctors said he'd develop faster at home." She could sense Jennifer's body stiffen. The tenuous camaraderie they'd developed evaporated like a morning mist.

"It's not catchy, for heaven's sake!"

Jennifer looked chagrined. "Well, I really didn't think it was . . . exactly. It's just that retarded people make me feel—weird."

They both gave unconscious sighs of relief when the auditorium, where the annual summer musical was rehearsed, came into sight. The sprawling brick building was quiet except for a few stragglers filing into the door nearest the music rooms.

Lexi had dreaded moving midsummer, fearing that she'd spend July and August alone, waiting for school to open to meet her classmates. But the musical brought kids her age together every day. That's where she'd met Jennifer, who had stood in the soprano section snapping gum and clowning, pretending to read a musical score upside down.

Now, as they scrambled for their places in the rehearsal hall, Lexi's eyes traveled across the bright moving color kaleidoscope of the cast. The kids wore everything from neon and Hawaiian prints to the plain brown uniform of the fast-food chain across the street from the school. Her gaze came to rest on the men's tenor section.

Jennifer's gaze must have followed the same path, for she leaned close to Lexi's ear and whispered, "Hunk section. The one with the lifeguard tan is Jerry Randall. I'd give anything to go out on a date with him."

Jerry had his arms crossed over his chest in a look-at-me pose and his feet propped on the chair in front of him—much to the dismay of a small, nervous-looking boy who didn't quite know how to reclaim his seat.

Lexi rolled her eyes toward Jennifer. Jerry *was* nice looking. But she liked the looks of the blond boy three chairs down. He smiled easily and his dark blue T-shirt matched his eyes.

Mrs. Waverly, the director, her beige curls bobbing on top of her head, tapped her baton on a music stand. "All right, everyone. We're ready to begin. I'd like to start by having you turn to page—" Mrs. Waverly's words were interrupted by a flurry of activity at the door. Three girls engaged in high-pitched laughter strolled into the room, oblivious to the malevolent glare of the director.

Jennifer whistled through her teeth. "Hi-Five strikes again."

Lexi stared at the girl blankly. "Hi-Five?"

"You mean you haven't heard of them yet?" Jennifer hissed through clenched teeth. "Boy, are you ever new in town!"

The cast of Cedar River's summer musical sank into theatrical silence, waiting to see what would happen next.

"Young ladies, you are late and you are rude. Please take your places. Now." Mrs. Waverly gripped the edges of the music rack until her knuckles whitened.

The three girls returned Mrs. Waverly's level gaze. Their eyes locked and the minute hand of the clock seemed to stand still. Then the tallest, a redhead, appeared about to speak. Just as Lexi was sure Mrs. Waverly was going to crack under the insolent stare-down, the redhead announced, "Sure, Teach. Why not?"

Lexi could hear the corporate sigh of relief as the group relaxed. After its rocky beginning, rehearsal moved ahead rapidly. Mrs. Waverly gave no one a moment for the renewal of the girls' earlier antics. Still, after the practice, Lexi felt washed out from the tension.

"What was going on in there, anyway?" she demanded of Jennifer as they hurried down the hall.

"Oh, those girls belong to Hi-Five. They just like to stir things up once in a while. It's never boring around them." Jennifer's voice held a distinct note of admiration.

"You *liked* the way they were acting?" Lexi asked incredulously. She thought they'd been very disrespectful.

Still, there *was* something more about those girls—a confidence, a poise—that *was* very exciting. Even Lexi, who'd been known for having her fair share of escapades in her old hometown, felt like a brown sparrow next to those bright, flashy Hi-Five canaries.

"They dare to do things no one else does. They're the most popular crowd in school. I mean, if you're a Hi-Five you're really *in*." Jennifer didn't disguise the awe in her voice.

Lexi had been popular in her former home, but she'd certainly never behaved like that. "They're all very pretty," Lexi ventured, not yet sure what to make of this information she was receiving.

"You bet. Pretty and popular. I'm up for membership in the club. If I get in, *then* Jerry Randall will ask me out. I hope I make it!" Jennifer forgot to snap her gum, she was so engrossed in the thought of becoming a Hi-Fiver.

"That reminds me. Who was the good-looking guy about three chairs down—blond, tan, wearing a Twins T-shirt?"

"That's Todd Winston. He's a doll, but no one will ever pull him away from all the sports he plays or his summer jobs long enough to get a date with him." Jennifer waved a hand in the air.

"What kind of job does he have?"

"I dunno, exactly," Jennifer shrugged. "He works for his mom part of the time. She's a bigwig administrator for something. And his brother owns a garage on Tenth Street. He works there too. Why? Do you have your eye on Todd Winston?"

"No, silly. I'm new, remember? I have the right to be curious." Didn't Jennifer ever think of anything but boys?

"Okay, but just remember, Jerry Randall and Todd Winston are both out of reach for us mere mortals. If a Hi-Five doesn't get them, no one will."

"How do you get to be a Hi-Five, anyway? What makes it all so special and exclusive?" Lexi was tucking this information away for future reference.

"*They* decide on *you*. You can't join unless they ask you. Only so many can be Hi-Fivers at a time. They've set a membership limit. Three graduated this summer and will be replaced before school starts in the fall. They interview prospective members and then pick whom they want. I got interviewed last week."

"When will you know?"

"When they want to tell me." Jennifer's enthusiasm dimmed for a moment. "They aren't all that nice to anyone who doesn't belong to the group. But they'll be nice to me once I'm in. It's a ticket to popularity, Lexi. If they ever want to interview you, don't pass it up."

"I'm not sure that would ever happen, Jennifer." Or, she added to herself, if she'd even want them to. "I'm brand new in town. Miss Nobody. Why would they ask me?"

"To keep up interest. Guys like the new girl in town. You'd probably be good for the club!"

It all sounded very complicated and not quite right, Lexi mused. But as lonesome as she'd been these past days, even the Hi-Five sounded appealing.

"Just remember, if you *do* get an interview, don't go and blow it!"

"Blow it? How would I do that?"

"By mentioning, well . . . you know. I mean, it just wouldn't be a good idea. Unnecessary and all that," Jennifer stammered.

"Mentioning *what*? What might keep me from getting into the Hi-Five?" Lexi demanded, her curiosity piqued.

Jennifer lowered her head and her voice. Her answer seemed to come from inside the collar of her shirt. "Ben."

"What?"

"Your brother." Jennifer's face flushed as red as the cherry-colored stripe in her blouse. "I wouldn't mention Ben, that's all. They might not like it that you had . . . well, you know."

"A retarded brother?" Lexi's soft voice sharpened in anger.

"Yeah. They might not like that. You understand, don't you?"

Suddenly Lexi was anxious to be home—to see Ben.

"I've got to go, Jennifer. See you tomorrow at practice?"

"Sure. See ya." Lexi could hear Jennifer's gum begin to pop and snap as the girl walked away. Lexi's eyes clouded slightly.

She momentarily forgot that she'd been uprooted from her lifelong home and friends. She ceased to remember her father's new clinic. She left behind the memory of Ben's teary cheeks and trembling lower lip. Instead, she remembered the first day her parents brought her little brother home from the hospital.

"Ohhhh!" Her lips had puckered in delight as the fat cherub swaddled in receiving blankets had clutched her outstretched finger. "Mommy, he's so *special!*"

Mrs. Leighton's eyes had clouded, much as Lexi's had now. "You're right, Lexi. Our Benjamin *is* special. More special than you know."

That was the first time Lexi heard the phrase "Down's syndrome." Those words were to alter her life forever after, but that early afternoon in June, when she was only seven, nothing was so important as her brand-new beautiful baby brother.

"Our baby has Down's syndrome, Lexi," her mother had persisted.

"What's that?" Lexi had pulled herself away from Ben's soft, round cheeks long enough to inquire. Why was her mother so serious, anyway?

"It means that Ben won't grow up to be just like the rest of us, Lexi. Ben was born with what is called a genetic imbalance. I know this is something you can't understand right now, but you will as you get older."

"But what *is* it?" Lexi had insisted on knowing.

"It's a mistake in Ben's genes." Seeing Lexi's befuddled look, Mrs. Leighton had struggled on. "Chromosomes are such tiny things that you can't see them unless you're a scientist with a powerful microscope. Ben and children like him have chromosomes that are arranged in special ways. This arrangement is called Down's syndrome. That extra little chromosome is going to make Ben different from the rest of our family. He's not going to grow up to be like you, Lexi. There are going to be some things about Ben that will set him apart from other children his age."

"Like what?" Lexi could still recall the knotting sensations of uncertainty and fear deep in her belly. Uncertainty and fear. They were chasing away all the good feelings she had looking at this wonderful baby. What was her mother getting at, anyway?

"He won't be able to go to the same school as you, Lexi. He'll need more help to learn the things that come easy for you."

"So? We started cursive writing and I'm having trouble with that. Maybe he'll be good at cursive."

"I'm afraid not, honey. Ben just won't be able to grow up to be like you." Lexi remembered the soft, sad look in her mother's eyes.

"But I don't *want* him to grow up to be just like me! You said I shouldn't want to be just like everyone else, that I should be myself. I want him to grow up to be *Ben*! I love Ben just the way he is. It doesn't matter what he can learn and what he can't," Lexi had retorted. She had been relieved to see the grimness around her mother's eyes vanish.

"Out of the mouths of babes," Mrs. Leighton had murmured more to herself than to Lexi.

"What does that mean, Mom?"

"Just that you've spoken some very wise words for a seven-year-old, Lexi. Words I'm going to remember. And we're all going to love Ben *just the way he is*."

And she did love Ben for the special little person that he was. Smiling to herself, Lexi increased her pace and headed for home.

"Well, dear, how was music practice?" Mrs. Leighton inquired over the lid of the box she was emptying.

"Okay."

"Just okay? Didn't you meet any new kids today either?"

"There were lots at practice," Lexi murmured, thinking of the Hi-Five.

"Good! I knew you'd make friends easily, Lexi. You had so many in your last school, I knew it wouldn't take you long to find new ones."

"It's not like back home, Mom." Lexi pulled up a stool and watched her mother unload the last of the packing boxes.

"Of course not. I know I sound like a broken record, but this is home now, and it will be as good."

"I'm not so sure of that," Lexi muttered.

Mrs. Leighton pushed the box aside and sat down across the counter from her daughter. "Whatever is making you so negative today?"

"I hate it here," she blurted. "I really do! Everyone already has friends. They don't need me. Anyway, they aren't going to want anything to do with me when they find out that I have a retarded brother."

"Nonsense. You've never worried before about what other people thought. Why start now?" Mrs. Leighton squared her slim shoulders defiantly as she always did when there was any threat or harsh word about Ben.

Lexi sighed. Her mother hadn't heard Jennifer's words. Her mother hadn't seen how flashy and confident those Hi-Five girls had been or felt the waves of unfamiliar self-doubt that washed over her. Her mother didn't know all the dreadful questions she had about why God had allowed Ben to be born as he was. Her mother wouldn't believe that either of her children was less than wonderful. But Lexi didn't feel very wonderful at that moment.

A small sound caught her attention and she turned toward the doorway leading to the dining room.

"Hi, Lexi!" Ben, barefoot and shirtless, stood in the arch, clutching a blanket.

"Hi, Ben. Did you just wake up from your nap?" An unwilling smile tweaked the corners of her lips.

"Nap." Ben had a way of repeating the last or most important word of a sentence when he was in agreement. Even if he'd remained silent, Lexi could tell by the sleepy squint to his almond-shaped eyes and the spikes of dark hair that stood up in clumps all over his head.

Then Ben smiled. Their father always said that if Ben's smile could be translated into watts, it would light Chicago. That radiant, delighted-to-see-you smile was beaming on Lexi. Her heart jerked hard in her chest and she opened her arms.

Ben barrelled into her welcoming embrace with the force of a steam engine and nuzzled his head against her shoulder. He smelled like fresh soap and sunshine.

"Did you play outside before your nap, Ben?"

"Outside."

Ben's chubby fingers traveled across Lexi's face, studying the planes. That voltage-bright smile faded. She could tell he had something on his mind.

"Lexi left."

"I know, Ben. I had to practice for the summer musical. I'm going to sing. It's a good chance to meet some new friends here in Cedar River."

"Friends," Ben nodded sagely. He knew full well the value of friends. He'd been forced to move away from all of his.

Friends. Lexi's mind traveled to the people she'd been exposed to today. Jennifer, of course. The Hi-Five girls. Jerry Randall. And Todd Winston, the nice-looking blond boy who was too busy for dates. Lexi sighed. After always being in the center of things, it was no picnic to be new and alone.

Why had her parents told her it would be fun to be the new girl in town? If it was fun, why did she feel so wretchedly miserable? She hadn't wanted to start over. She'd liked it where she was. She'd had lots of friends at both church and school. Everyone knew her there. And everyone knew Ben.

"Lexi?" His voice was soft and inquiring near her ear.

She smiled and lifted him to the floor. "Come on, Ben. Let's go play ball." She was rewarded with the high-beam smile and a small warm hand tucked eagerly into her palm. Even if she was unhappy, she could still manage to fill the void in Ben's social life. She and Ben both had best friends that would never abandon them—each other.

By the end of the week Lexi began to think she had been wrong about their unfailing devotion. And it was she who had become the traitor.

Jennifer Golden had been accepted by the Hi-Five.

Lexi had known it immediately when she walked into rehearsal on Thursday. Jennifer—instead of slouching across her seat, feet tucked into the chair ahead of her—stood, shoulders square and proud, in the center of a group of laughing girls.

The transformation was amazing. Her tan seemed darker, her hair more blond, her smile more dazzling. Lexi shook her head slightly. It was apparent that being accepted had done wonders for Jennifer's confidence.

But it had done nothing for Jennifer's budding relationship with Lexi. Suddenly, Lexi's one acquaintance was too busy for anything but hasty greetings and hurried conversations when no other club member was around.

"Jennifer, I never get to see you anymore!" Lexi was quick to point out as the practice session ended.

"I know. I'm sorry, but I've gotta go. I'm supposed to meet Minda and Tressa at the Hamburger Shack at four. They're planning my initiation into Hi-Five."

"Okay. See you sometime." Lexi had a difficult time keeping the disappointment from her voice.

"Lexi . . ." Jennifer paused and turned back to study her friend. "I'm not supposed to tell you this, but the girls are considering asking you to interview. If they do, remember what I said. *Don't mention Ben.*"

"But—"

"Just do as I say, Lexi. Then we can be together again. Don't mess up by telling them about your brother." Jennifer scooped her music books and equipment from the chair. "Ben's a cute enough kid. Let them find out for themselves . . . later. Bye."

Thoughtfully, Lexi leaned against the cinderblock wall. Had she and her parents done something to deserve this? Was it some kind of punishment from God? It was certainly beginning to feel like it.

Still, she began to imagine what it would be like to be a Hi-Fiver. Popular. Busy. No longer alone. Jerry Randall. Todd Winston.

"Hi!" The voice broke into Lexi's daydream, making her jump. Her fantasy had come to life. Before her, legs widespread, thumbs dug deep into the circle of his belt, stood Jerry Randall.

"Oh! You startled me!" Lexi blushed to the roots of her golden blond hair. "I mean, hello."

Jerry's smile flashed in the sunlight. "Sorry. Whatcha thinking about?"

Lexi's blush heightened. It would be rather difficult to explain that she'd been thinking of *him*. "Nothing really. Just daydreaming."

"From the rumors I've been hearing, you won't have time for that much longer." Jerry hunkered down in front of her, balancing his elbows on his knees.

"And what's that supposed to mean?" she challenged.

"Oh, nothing. Just some gossip I heard hanging around the Hamburger Shack." Jerry gave a lopsided grin that curled into an almost sneer.

"And what kind of gossip was that?"

"That the girls in High-Five wanted to interview you. New girl in town and all that. I thought I'd get a head start. By the way, my name is Jerry Randall— and I already know you're Alexis Leighton."

"Yes—um—nice to meet you, Jerry."

Lexi recalled what Jennifer had said. Hi-Five was the fastest, surest way to make friends here in Cedar River. Boys like Jerry and Todd Winston liked the girls in the club. As much as she resented Jennifer's warning about mentioning Ben, suddenly the prospects of being a member seemed very appealing.

"I'm not sure the Hi-Five group will ever interview me."

"Pretty as you are? It's a sure thing." Jerry uncoiled himself from the squatting position and stood.

Lexi, unwilling to let him move away too quickly, inquired, "Do you like being in the musical, Jerry?"

"Me? Nah. But it's something to do." He angled himself against the wall. "How do you like Cedar River?"

"Well, I haven't met too many people yet. Seems like everyone is involved with summer jobs or their friends."

"Guess I'll just have to take you around and do some introductions, then." He threw his head back with a confident air. "I know just about everybody in school."

"Tha—that would be very nice." So this is what happened when it was even suspected that someone might be Hi-Five material!

"Okay. Today's Thursday. Want to go to a movie on Saturday? Everyone is going to be there."

"Sure. Fine. Do you know where I live?" Suddenly Lexi was afraid she wouldn't remember her own new address.

"I've got to work at the Hamburger Shack until seven-thirty that night. Do you mind just meeting me at the Shack?"

"All right. What time?"

"Seven forty-five. I'll clean up there and be ready for you. See you then!"

As Jerry sauntered off, Lexi followed him with her eyes. Then she pinched herself hard.

"Ouch!" she yelped. So it *was* true. She hadn't been dreaming. She had a date for Saturday night.

"Lexi's home!" Ben sang. "Lexi's home!" He'd obviously been sitting on the porch steps for some time. He'd arranged every button in his mother's button box in neat, symmetrical rows by size and color—a job that must have taken a good share of his afternoon. Though there were occasional mistakes—blue buttons in with black, or large buttons in the midst of small ones—he'd gotten most of them right. Ben had an uncanny eye for color and symmetry and supreme patience.

Ben was the most complete and loving little human being she'd ever known. Why couldn't others see that?

"Hi, Benjamin. Have you been playing with buttons all afternoon?"

She scooted down beside him on the porch step.

"Buttons." He nodded and ran a gentle finger over the rows.

"Should I help you put the buttons away?"

"Away."

As the two bent over their work, Mrs. Leighton walked onto the porch.

"Hello, Lexi. Did you have a good time at rehearsal today?"

"Yeah. Fine."

"Just fine?"

"Well, more than fine, actually. I got asked out on a date."

"Anybody I know?" Mrs. Leighton sank onto the top step with her children.

"Really, Mother. How could it be? You don't know any boys in Cedar River!"

"I suppose that's true. Is he nice?" Mrs. Leighton smiled, undaunted.

"I think so. He's in the musical."

"I'm glad you're finally making some friends, Lexi. I've been worried about you."

"You have?" Lexi was surprised. She didn't think her mother had had time to notice her lately.

"You've been alone so much since we moved. It's not healthy. You used to be with friends every moment you could. I'd like to see you get involved with girls your own age."

Hi-Five.

But would her mother like it if she knew that one of the requirements for joining the group was to keep Ben a secret—even for a little while?

It was just too confusing. She'd been trying to pray about the situation, but she hardly knew what she should be praying for—friends? wisdom? What did she need most? She knew one thing she needed for sure, and that was to spend more time looking for answers in her Bible.

Before she could speak, Mrs. Leighton jumped to her feet. "I've got potatoes boiling on the stove. Get Ben washed up and come and eat. And Lexi . . . I'm glad you're finding some friends. Dad and I knew you would."

But, Lexi continued to worry; would her mother be so pleased if she knew more about Hi-Five? Would they really, as Jennifer had warned, reject her if they knew about Ben? Still, they were the most popular girls in school. Jerry Randall was proof of that. Just being considered for the club had encouraged him to ask her out.

Confused and torn, Lexi made her way into the house for supper. Maybe Jennifer had been wrong. Maybe the Hi-Five wasn't considering her at all. Maybe her loneliness would last the rest of the summer.

Chapter Two

"Lexi, will you take Ben uptown with you? I've got to get this unpacking finished and he insists on being underfoot." Marilyn Leighton brushed damp curls back from her forehead as she peered around the corner at her daughter. "Please?"

"But, Mom! I wanted to get a new blouse for tonight. I can't shop with Ben," Lexi protested. She wanted something in pale pink, to go with her grandmother's pearl necklace. She hadn't had time to sew anything and she certainly didn't need a little brother poking along behind.

"Ben will behave. Have him take a toy to play with. I can't stand living in this mess any longer. I want the last of the packing boxes out of the house by suppertime. Now scram, both of you."

"Come on, Ben," Lexi acquiesced. "And bring your little car that makes into a robot."

Obediently Ben picked up his toys and followed Lexi. His distinctive rambling gait slowed him slightly.

Still irritated, Lexi kept him a step or two behind

until she heard his small voice.

"Lexi mad?"

Lexi spun around. Ben's lower lip was trembling and a crystal tear was poised on the bottom rim of each dark eye. He was struggling with a toy in each hand, trying to master them in one fist so the thumb of the other could go into its comforting position in his mouth.

"Oh, Ben! I'm not mad at you! Come 'ere, little fellow. Let me put those toys in my pocket. Then you and that thumb can get together if you want to."

"Thumb." Ben looked at it distastefully once his hands were free of toys. He grabbed Lexi's hand.

She sighed. It wasn't his fault their family had moved. He was as confused, lonely, and lost as she. Blaming him wouldn't help.

Still, by day's end, Lexi wished she'd never agreed to take Ben uptown.

Lexi was intent on trying on every size-five blouse in the store. She momentarily forgot Ben, who had ensconced himself in the center of a three-way mirror and busied himself making faces into the glass.

Lexi stepped from the dressing room to view her reflection.

"How do you like this one, Ben? It's pretty, isn't—" Lexi paused to look around. "Ben? Benjamin! Where are you?" A knot of panic tightened around her stomach.

Ben was gone. "May I help you?" A salesclerk with glasses dangling from a chain around her neck inquired. "Are you looking for someone?"

"My little brother. He was here just a minute ago—sitting in front of the mirror. Have you seen him?" She struggled to keep the alarm from her voice. Ben had no sense of direction whatsoever. Once he was out of her sight, he had no way of knowing how to find her again.

"How old is this child and what does he look like?" Lexi could hear a hint of disapproval in the older woman's voice.

"He's eight. He's got dark brown hair and brown almond-shaped eyes and he's short for his age and he's wearing red shorts and a red-and-white striped T-shirt."

"Well, he shouldn't be too difficult to find," the clerk assured her.

"And he's mentally retarded."

"Oh." The woman's voice changed. "Well, then, I'll begin looking while you get dressed. He wouldn't get on an elevator, would he?"

Lexi swallowed. Ben liked nothing better than buttons to push. She spun into the dressing room and pulled on her clothes.

They scoured the entire third floor of the department store, but Ben was nowhere to be seen. Lexi, fighting to remain calm, announced, "He must have found the elevator or the stairs. I'd better check the other floors."

"And I'll call the house detective. We wouldn't want him to wander out of the store and into the street." The clerk bustled off, oblivious to the terror she'd fanned in Lexi.

Tears were stinging at the backs of Lexi's eyes as she reached the second floor of the building. She prayed frantically as she scanned the aisles. The thought of Ben beneath the wheels of a car was too much to bear. A wave of resentment and bitterness washed over her. If Ben were like other kids, then this might never have happened. Before she had time to carry the thought further, the sound of giggling attracted Lexi's attention.

A group of teenaged girls were clustered in a semicircle around a display in the toy department. They were snickering and pointing at something in the exhibit. With a mixed sense of dread and relief, Lexi made her way to the group.

They were looking at a toy train display. The automated wonder chugged up plastic hills and down cardboard valleys. It careened under artificial bridges and through paper tunnels. Operating this elaborate train setup from a perch at the center of the display was Ben. Gleefully he punched buttons on the control board, making the train speed up or grind to a halt. He chortled every time the little train took an unexpected trip along a side track and clapped his hands when it peeked out from the end of a tunnel. Under one arm he clasped a teddy bear, its price tags hanging limply from one ear. Ben had made himself right at home.

"Have you ever seen anything so *funny*?" one of the girls in the cluster giggled.

"I think he's darling!" another cooed.

"Yeah, but isn't he big enough to *know* better?"

"Maybe he's—"

Not able to stand any more and not wanting to hear what this group of girls thought of her brother, Lexi pushed her way through the group to stand before Ben.

"Hi, Lexi! Train!" Ben beamed that high-watt

smile Lexi's way, but, for once, it didn't melt her.

Furious, relieved and embarrassed, Lexi's voice was unusually harsh. "Benjamin! You get out of there right now! Those are not your toys. You wandered off and scared me out of my wits! You are in big trouble. Just wait till you get home!" She stretched a hand to him and pulled him across the toy trains. The teddy bear tumbled from his arms and landed on the floor.

The cluster of girls backed quickly away, some hiding their amused mouths behind concealing hands. Lexi could hear muffled laughter as she towed Ben toward the exit.

Perhaps those were some of the girls from her new school—girls who might have become her friends! Now they were laughing at her and Ben. He'd ruined everything for her!

"Lexi mad?"

She'd almost forgotten that she had the guilty party in tow. With a twinge of remorse, she loosened her grip on Ben's fingers. The tips had turned bright pink with the pressure of her hand. He stumbled and she grabbed him by one elbow for support.

"Lexi?" His voice was a frightened whisper.

"You shouldn't have wandered off like that, Ben. You got yourself lost."

"Lost?"

She could read the puzzlement in his eyes. Lexi sighed. Ben hadn't felt lost. He'd known exactly where he was. In his mind, he hadn't done a thing wrong.

Little did he know, Lexi thought. She was sure she'd never forget the looks of amusement and pity in those girls' eyes. Perhaps Jennifer was right. Perhaps there *was* a stigma involved in being Ben's sister. It hadn't mattered in Grover's Point. They'd both been born there. Everyone knew about Ben. Everyone loved him. Here, though, people laughed and stared at Ben—and at her.

Lexi could almost taste the resentment she felt toward those girls for laughing. And, for the first time in her life, she felt resentment toward Ben.

"Did you find a new blouse, Lexi?" her mother asked when they entered the kitchen door.

"No."

Mrs. Leighton spun around at Lexi's one-syllable answer. "What happened to you two? Have you been crying?" She clutched a teary Ben close to her body and put her other hand on Lexi's shoulder.

"Lost." Ben explained mournfully, the tears finally spilling onto his T-shirt.

"What?"

"He wandered off while I was trying on blouses. I even had the house detective looking for him. It was awful!"

"Well, where did you find him, then?"

"In the center of a toy train display, running the trains and clutching a teddy bear."

Marilyn suppressed a smile. "Well, I guess it worked out all right, then."

"No, it didn't! It didn't work out at all!" Her anger spilled out. "He made a fool of me in front of a whole bunch of girls! They were wondering what was wrong with Ben. And they'll wonder what's wrong with me, too!"

"That's nonsense, Lexi," Mrs. Leighton frowned.

"No, it isn't! They were laughing at us!"

"People just don't think things through very well sometimes, honey. You have to remember that."

"It's easy for you! You have Dad! I don't have anyone in this horrible new town!" Lexi ran to her room and slammed the door. The anger and confusion she'd suffered since the move tore at her insides. She wanted to pray, to lay her troubles in God's open arms, but she felt hard and cold inside.

If this is a test, God, I've failed. I know I'm not as strong or as faithful as I should be. I don't understand why Ben is the way he is, and I don't understand why I have to be here where I'm so lonely. I just don't get it, God. Then the tears she'd tried to stem came pouring out. When her sobs finally eased, she could hear a tiny scrabbling at her door.

"Lexi's crying. Lexi's crying. Ben's here."

He'd come to comfort her. But today she didn't want Ben's comfort. She was sure nothing could ease that empty feeling she had inside. The thought came to her that she should read her Bible. She decided she would . . . later.

By seven o'clock Lexi had tried on every blouse in her closet. The emotional storm had subsided, but she and Ben were warily skirting each other's paths. Lexi felt guilty for her behavior, and Ben, always attuned to his sister's emotions, was behaving instinctively. He could sense that now was not a good time to get on Lexi's nerves.

"You look wonderful, darling! That's perfect for

tonight," Marilyn smiled. "I've always thought you looked good in pink."

The mirror did throw back a rather nice reflection, Lexi mused. The pale pink jeans and cotton sweater had been her birthday gift. She'd chosen to go conservative tonight, rather than one of the funky outfits she usually wore. Even her jewelry—a tiny rhinestone brooch—was more subdued than usual.

She'd brushed her long blond hair until it gleamed, and tied it back with a big pink bow tilted rakishly over one ear. She wore her best sandals and her mother's expensive perfume. There was nothing more she could do before she went to meet Jerry Randall at the Hamburger Shack.

"Lexi's beautiful!" Ben was playing on the top step of the porch as she left the house. He was in his swimming suit, dumping water from bucket to bucket. His sturdy little body gleamed in the evening light. He was so perfect—and yet so flawed. A deep, aching sense of unfairness washed over her. It just didn't make sense. Right now, nothing much did.

Shaking her head as if to shed off her melancholy thoughts, she gently ran a hand through Ben's soft hair. "You be good tonight, Ben."

He nodded solemnly and announced, "Ben won't get lost."

Lexi smiled in spite of herself. Maybe the day hadn't been a total waste after all. "And I hope the night's not wasted either," she murmured.

The Hamburger Shack was buzzing when Lexi entered. The hum abated for a moment as some of the more curious stopped talking to see who had entered.

She was relieved to see Jerry hurrying her way. She didn't want to spend any time alone being the object of someone's curiosity. She'd done enough of that for one day.

"Hi! Right on time. Ready to go?" Jerry was even more handsome than she'd remembered. He was wearing navy pants and a green and navy rugby shirt. His dark hair was damp and slicked back from his forehead. The green of the shirt brought out the green flecks in his eyes.

He appraised her looks with a practiced eye. Then he smiled. "You look nice." He lifted a finger and ran it across the rhinestone pin.

"It was my grandmother's," Lexi explained, even before the question was asked. "I collect costume jewelry. Old things."

Jerry nodded thoughtfully as he led her toward his car. Once inside the theater, Jerry bought the tickets while Lexi stood near his shoulder watching the crowd.

"Popcorn?" Jerry stuffed the ticket stubs into his pocket and nodded toward the concessions stand.

"Please." Lexi hadn't been able to choke down either lunch or supper. Now her stomach was beginning to make embarrassing noises. She pressed the palms of her hands against her growling stomach.

"Here." He shoved a tub of buttered popcorn her way. Jerry Randall wasn't much of a conversationalist, Lexi thought wryly, but tonight she wasn't either.

The darkness of the theater was a comforting blanket about her shoulders. There, Lexi could relax the pasted-on smile she'd been wearing since the

Hamburger Shack, and unobtrusively study her date.

He certainly didn't seem bent on conversation. Though she'd struggled to learn more about him on the way to the theater, he'd tended to answer in monosyllables and gutteral noises. And he'd never asked her a question about herself or her former school.

She was relieved when the previews rolled and unaccountably pleased when the movie ended. If quizzed, Lexi doubted that she could even have begun to describe the plot. They followed the crowd through the exit silently. Outside, in the parking lot, a large group had gathered.

"Hey! Randall! Come and look at Todd's new jalopy!"

Lexi scanned the scene, her gaze coming to rest on Todd Winston's blond head. He was leaning against the hood of an old car. Round-edged and hulking, the navy blue vehicle sat in the middle of a group of teenagers.

"What is it, anyway? Looks like a refugee from a salvage shop." Jerry sauntered toward the vehicle, leaving Lexi to catch up.

"It's a '49 Ford coupe. Runs like a charm. Don't you like it, Jerry?" Todd inquired, the expression on his face showing that he already knew the answer.

"Not much. Why don't you get a decent car once, Winston? You know, something than runs and looks like it was made in this decade? What's this thing you have about old junkers, anyway?"

"Antique cars, Jerry. Antique cars! Not old junkers. Just wait till I get this fixed up. It's going to be great." Todd smiled engagingly, this time including Lexi in his smile.

Her heart jerked about as if it was suspended on a puppeteer's strings. Lexi bit the inside of her cheek to prevent her from smiling too widely in return.

"Well, I don't know why you waste your time. Why bother with that when you could get something brand new?"

Todd shrugged cheerfully. "I like 'fixer-uppers.' We've got different tastes, that's all. World's big enough for both of us."

Lexi could sense the tension in Jerry's posture. He didn't like Todd Winston very well, that was obvious. Jealous? Maybe. Todd was certainly handsome, popular, and at ease in the big crowd. Suddenly Jerry took her hand and pulled her to his own vehicle.

New and full of plastic, it didn't have nearly the charm of Todd's old clunker. Lexi smiled to herself. What kind of boy was Todd Winston, anyway? She didn't know any others who bought antique cars. She liked that. It was like her passion for old jewelry. She didn't know many teenagers who liked anything old. Just two. Herself and Todd Winston.

As Jerry and Lexi pulled out of the parking lot, they drove past some familiar faces. Lexi scowled a bit trying to place them. Once she did, she slid downward on the seat until she was nearly invisible from outside the car.

The girls from the department store. No wonder they had peered so curiously into Jerry's car! The embarrassment returning, Lexi hardly realized that Jerry was speaking to her. He looked apologetic.

"I know this is crazy, but Dad called me at work and told me I had to go to the airport to pick up my aunt tonight. The plane gets in at eleven. I've got to take you home early. Sorry."

They hadn't talked at all! What kind of a date was this?

Then Jerry added, "I'll drop you off and come by tomorrow. We'll go out for ice cream or something. Kind of finish tonight's date. Okay?"

"That would be nice."

"Yeah, well, I hope it's all right. My aunt wasn't supposed to arrive till tomorrow, but . . ."

Her mood brightened. At least she'd have company to look forward to tomorrow. Lexi didn't even mind as Jerry opened her door from his side of the car and let her out at the street.

Lexi watched him drive off with a puzzled look. It was the oddest date she'd ever had. Especially since it was Todd Winston's face that stuck in her mind instead of Jerry's.

"Lunchtime, Lexi."

Lexi could feel Ben's fingers dancing lightly across her face as she lay in the sun. She'd hurried through breakfast and squirmed through Sunday morning church services just thinking about Jerry coming over this afternoon. Even the letter she'd written to her friend, Denise, had been filled with uncharacteristic restlessness.

It was odd, Lexi mused, but since her family's move, she'd been mixed up about so many things that she'd taken for granted in her old home—Ben's retardation, the meaning and value of friendship, the importance of God in her life right now. She reached for the lined writing pad next to her chair and read again the letter she'd composed.

Dear Denise,

You can't believe how quiet it is here. I'm anxious for school to start so at least I have somewhere to go. The musical I told you about is a real lifesaver. I don't know what I'd do without that. I really miss you and Cory. Ben misses you, too.

I've had more time to think since we've moved to Cedar River—more time than I've wanted. All I seem to come up with are more questions, though. Most of the questions have been about Ben.

Not very many people here know that I have a retarded brother. In Grover's Point, everybody knew Ben and they loved him almost as much as I do, but it's different here.

It's made me wonder: Why is Ben the way he is? I heard someone say once that kids like Ben made people appreciate their own health and that of their children a lot more. But that can't be part of God's plan—that's too high a price to pay so that someone can be thankful for his own health.

When I was little, I wondered if my parents had done something wrong. I figured that Ben's handicap was some kind of punishment for them, but that doesn't make sense either. Why should Ben have to suffer? He didn't do anything. He was just a baby.

Sorry this letter is getting so grim. It's just that nothing makes much sense to me right now. I wish you were here. Then we could have some fun.

That reminds me! I've got a date for this afternoon. His name is Jerry Randall and he's cute!

Better go. I've got some serious primping to do!

Love,
Lexi

She smiled as she reread the letter. Just writing her thoughts down had helped. She didn't have any answers, but the questions were clearer. Maybe things were going to improve after all. Things would be different today. She was sure of it. Jerry would be more talkative and so would she. She wouldn't feel like a new toy that Jerry was showing off here in her own home. And they could get to know each other and become friends. She could use a few friends right now.

"Lexi coming?" Ben leaned forward until his nose was a quarter inch away from hers.

"Yes, I'm coming, Ben. As soon as you let me up."

He scrambled off the lawn chair and landed with a small thud on the porch. Dusting off the seat of his pants, he smiled brightly at his sister. "Oops."

Laughing, Lexi scooped the dark-haired bundle into her arms. "Benjamin Leighton, you are the funniest, dearest little boy in the whole world."

"Whole world." Ben threw his arms wide to encompass Lexi.

Her eyes misted. Ben could so easily bring her to tears or laughter. Sometimes she loved him so much it hurt. Now that she had so many new things on her mind, it was easy to forget how much Ben depended on her. Best friends. That's what they were. Ben never forgot, even if she sometimes did.

"You're my best buddy, aren't you, Ben?"

"Best." And he gave her a bone-wrenching squeeze.

"Come on, you two," Mrs. Leighton called. "Lunch will be cold if you don't hurry. And, Lexi, didn't you say that someone was coming over this afternoon?"

"Jerry. He had to go to the airport to pick up his aunt, so he said he'd come over today and we could finish our date."

"What time is he coming?" her mother inquired as she moved a casserole from the oven to the table.

"I don't know exactly. He didn't say."

"Odd." Mrs. Leighton's brow wrinkled. "That seems a bit rude, not telling you when he'll arrive. That ties you up the entire afternoon."

"It's okay, Mom," Lexi defended him halfheartedly. "He probably knows I don't have any other friends here anyway."

"I don't like your attitude about that, Lexi. Where's your spunk? You'll have to get out and *make* some. I'm sure the church we've attended has a youth group. Join something. You know, get involved. Whatever happened to 'Let's not have a dull moment'?"

"Most of the church groups aren't meeting this summer and I'm already in the musical. But everyone comes and goes in pairs or groups." Lexi pushed the noodles into a pattern on her plate. "I think everyone and everything in this town must have been divided into pairs until I came along. It's like moving into Noah's ark." Crazy, impulsive, fun-loving Lexi Leighton. She wondered sometimes if that person had been left behind in the move.

"There must be another group to get involved with for the summer. Look around. You'll think of something. I know you."

Hi-Five. It kept cropping up in her thoughts. She'd be in with Jennifer again. Jerry Randall had asked her out after he'd heard they were considering her. If she joined, she'd have a group to be with when school started in the fall. Lexi also remembered what Jennifer had said about Todd Winston. "Jerry Randall and Todd Winston are out of reach for us. They're friendly only with girls who belong to Hi-Five."

Lexi felt a little traitorous waiting for Jerry and thinking about Todd, but she hadn't really liked the way Jerry had dropped her off in the street instead of walking her to the door. His looks were much nicer than his manners.

"Handsome is as handsome does," her grandmother had always said. Grandma would quote that verse in Matthew: "Imposters! You clean the outside of your cup and plate, while the inside is full of things you have gotten by violence and selfishness. . . . Clean what is inside the cup first, and then the outside will be clean too!"

Somehow, the passage seemed to fit where Jerry Randall was concerned. If a person's heart and mind weren't in good order, it didn't matter how popular or outwardly attractive a person was. What's inside a person is what really counts. Lexi wondered what Jerry was truly like—inside.

Before she could consider it any further, the telephone rang.

"Alexis, it's me, Jennifer!"

"Hi, Jennifer."

"Well, how was it?"

"How was what?"

"Your date with Jerry Randall! What else? The girls were pretty impressed that he asked you out before they'd even approached you about being in the club." Jennifer's voice was filled with awe. "That's a point for you."

"I didn't know I was supposed to be making points," Lexi murmured softly.

"Well, having Jerry Randall as a friend makes big points, believe me. Are you going to see him again?"

"He's coming over this afternoon." Lexi didn't feel like going into the facts behind the aborted date.

"Awright! We'll be in Hi-Five together in no time if you keep this up. Gotta go. Catch you later. Bye."

Lexi stared at the humming receiver distastefully. Whatever happened to friends you just made by accident? To having things in common with others? In Cedar River, having friends was an occupation you worked at, a career. Some people had status careers like the Hi-Five; others had blue-collar types.

Things weren't simple here in Cedar River.

Just as Lexi was about to give up on Jerry ever appearing, the doorbell rang.

He stood at the door, tall and tan, with damp dark hair slicked back across his head. Here and there a stray tendril escaped, curling at the nape of his neck.

"Hi! Were you waiting for me?"

Waiting? Lexi had been clinging to the overstuffed chair in the living room for three hours, peering out the window. Ben had tried to pry her away with games and she'd shooed him off. Now, when she'd finally resigned herself to the fact he wasn't coming, Jerry arrived. "Kind of," she admitted. "Come on in."

Lexi scanned the living room as they entered. She'd never before been concerned about her home being nice enough, but she was today. The furniture was elegant but worn. Her family always bought nice things but they used them well. There was no place in the house that was off limits to her or Ben—and sometimes things had gotten a little tattered or stained from use.

Everything seemed acceptable to Jerry, who threw himself onto the couch. "Nice place. Sorry I'm late. I decided to go swimming and forgot about the time."

Swimming? Lexi loved to swim. Why hadn't he asked her to go along instead of keeping her waiting here at home?

Before she could reply, Jerry continued. "So, tell me about where you came from, Lexi. North Dakota? Is that right?"

She nodded eagerly and began to speak. "It was just a little place. Lots of rural people and"—Jerry's eyes roamed over the room. He wasn't listening at all—"and we had a lot of trouble with buffalo eating out of our grocery sacks. That's something you have to put up with when you live on the prairie," Lexi concluded. Jerry never batted an eyelash.

Jerry seemed to lack in manners what he made up for in looks, she observed. Then Jerry disarmed her with his smile. "You're a really cute kid, Lexi. I think you'll get along just fine in Cedar River. We—"

His conversation stumbled to a halt as Ben came racing into the room. Ben wore a plastic fireman's hat on his head and carried a piece of vacuum cleaner hose. He was making swooshing water noises and dousing imaginary flames. Ben ground to a stop in front of the couch and stared curiously at Jerry.

"This is my little brother Ben. He's eight." Lexi hoped fervently that Ben wouldn't do anything silly.

"Hi, kid. I have an eight-year-old brother, too. Maybe you'll be in the same class at school next year." Jerry squinted a bit, trying to get a good look at Ben's face under the fireman's hat.

"Ahmm, I don't think so," Lexi said softly.

"What did you say?"

"I don't think Ben and your little brother will be in the same class at school next year. Ben's in the special education class."

"You mean he's—" Jerry stiffened and edged backward on the couch.

"Ben has Down's syndrome."

"Doesn't that mean he's retarded or something?" Jerry appeared extremely ill-at-ease.

"Yes. But Ben is only mildly affected. He has what's called mosaicism. He doesn't have all the characteristics of Down's syndrome, just some of them." Lexi wanted to reassure him, but Jerry's wary expression was deepening. "He has good motor skills and language. He's very trainable. His teachers expect that he'll be able to read someday."

"I didn't think people like that could ever do anything!" Jerry commented in disbelief.

" 'People like that' can do more than you can imagine," Lexi protested coolly. "My parents hope that he'll someday hold a paying job and live in a group home or monitored apartment. You're a good little worker, aren't you, Ben?"

"Good!" Ben beamed his light-bulb smile and moved toward his sister.

Jerry stood as Ben moved away from him. He shifted his weight uneasily from one foot to the other.

"I gotta be going now, Lexi."

"But you just came!"

"Ah, yeah, but . . . my aunt wanted to visit with

me! I promised I'd spend some time with her. So I really have to leave." Jerry backed toward the front door. Raising his hand in a limp farewell, he added, "We'll see ya . . . around."

He was gone.

Lexi sank disconsolately onto the chair. She knew why he'd run off so quickly. It was because of Ben.

Jerry was like so many people she'd met—afraid of being around retarded people. Afraid that some of what those poor individuals had might "rub off" on themselves.

How many others like Jerry were there in Cedar River? Would she have to keep Ben a secret if she was going to make friends? Was this all part of a dirty trick God was playing on her and her family? Hating herself for that thought and for the gnawing loneliness she felt inside, Lexi wept.

Ben, his expressive eyes revealing the hurt he felt for his big sister, sat at her side, smoothing her soft blond hair and making comforting sing-song noises until dusk fell over the Leighton household.

Chapter Three

The phone didn't ring for Lexi the rest of the week. Feigning disinterest, Lexi convinced her mother that she wasn't up to attending music rehearsal. She assured her parents that since she was only in the chorus, and not singing a solo part, she'd never be missed. Lexi was beginning to believe that if she dropped off the face of the earth, no one would notice. She'd even quit drawing designs and sewing. What did it matter? She had nowhere to go that called for a new outfit.

Then Tressa Williams called.

"Hello, Lexi? This is Tressa."

"Uh, hello." Lexi's surprise left her stammering.

"I'm a friend of Jennifer Golden's. I'm also the president of the Hi-Five club. Jennifer said she told you about us."

"A little bit." Lexi didn't want to reveal how much Jennifer had said. She remembered Tressa as the redhead who'd caused the disturbance at Mrs. Waverly's rehearsal.

"We'd like to come over and meet you, Lexi. And

get to know you better. It's just possible that you'd be right for membership in our club. Are you doing anything this afternoon?"

Am I doing anything this afternoon? Lexi choked back a wry laugh. She hadn't done anything all week except play quiet games with Ben. He was delighted with this change in his sister, having her all to himself. Lexi must have played a million games of Old Maid in the six days since Jerry Randall left the house like he'd been catapulted from a cannon.

Aloud, she answered, "Nothing special. I'm here alone. My family went shopping and won't be back until after supper."

"Great! We'll be right over."

After she hung up the receiver, Lexi began to wonder what she'd gotten herself into now. But she was excited. It had been a long, boring week. She'd known instinctively that Jerry Randall wouldn't call again. Not after the way he'd reacted to Ben. Sheer embarrassment at his insensitivity should have kept him away—if he'd even realized how badly he'd acted.

Lexi slipped into a pale blue jumpsuit she'd made and braided her hair in a single long plait that swung over one shoulder. She tied a powdery blue ribbon at the end of the braid and slicked a glimmer of lip gloss across her lips. If the Hi-Five didn't like what they saw, it wasn't because she hadn't tried.

When the doorbell rang, Lexi took a deep breath. Here it was, her chance to be a part of something in Cedar River. After the long, dreary week she'd just spent, she didn't want to make any mistakes.

When she opened the door, Jennifer Golden sauntered in, followed by the girls Lexi knew to be Tressa Williams and Minda Hannaford.

"Welcome to Cedar River, Lexi!" Tressa beamed.

Lexi blinked. Why hadn't someone said that to her weeks ago?

"Thanks."

"We're just here to visit. To get to know you. How do you like Cedar River so far?"

Not wanting to lie and knowing the truth would get her nowhere, Lexi dodged. "It's very pretty here. Lots more trees and lakes than back in North Dakota."

"That's not exactly what I meant," Tressa giggled. "I'm just assuming that you'd like it here after you started meeting the guys." She smiled slyly.

Was that all the girls in this town thought about? Boys? Jerry Randall was cropping up *again*. Apparently he hadn't told anyone of his near miss with the new girl and her strange little brother. Lexi chewed on her bottom lip.

"I really haven't put many names and faces together yet, but I'd like to meet more people." Lexi saw Jennifer nodding eagerly behind Tressa and Minda's backs. Apparently that was the kind of answer these girls wanted to hear.

It was nearly six o'clock when the threesome departed and Lexi was smiling as widely as the rest.

"I'll call you later," Jennifer promised as they descended the porch steps.

Lexi nodded and waved. It had felt wonderful to have a house full of girls again. They were nicer than she'd expected. Perhaps the image she had formed in her mind of the Hi-Five wasn't quite accurate. Deep inside, Lexi was hoping they'd ask her to join.

And the subject of Ben hadn't even come up.

It was Todd Winston who temporarily made Lexi forget her dream about joining the Hi-Five when his "antique" car broke down right in front of the Leightons' house.

Lexi, in the kitchen fixing her supper, heard the doorbell ring again. Dusting her free hand on the thigh of her jumpsuit, she threw open the door. She stood there mesmerized by a very greasy, very handsome Todd Winston.

"Well, hello there! I didn't know this was going to be *your* doorbell I was ringing!" His face creased in a wide grin. His teeth shown white against the background of suntan and motor oil.

"Hi, yourself," Lexi managed. "Can I help you?"

"My car broke down at the end of your driveway. My older brother owns a garage on Tenth Street. Could I use your phone to have him come and tow me home?"

"Sure. Come on in." Lexi fingered the ribbon in her hair.

Todd clumped past her in heavy work boots. His white T-shirt had seen better days. Splatters of oil and streaks of dirt gave it a muddy, tie-dyed look. He'd rolled up the sleeves to the shoulders, revealing thick muscular arms. The shirt was pulled out of the back of his jeans and dangling free. The knees of his jeans were patched and repatched. There was even a mended scrap of faded red on the seat of his pants. His streaky blond hair was tousled by the wind and restless fingers making trails through it. His face lit up in an engaging smile. "You're Lexi, aren't you?"

Lexi had never realized that four words could sound so sweet. He knew who she was. He'd taken the time to find out! But, unless she could manage to find some words to say in the dizzy, delighted whirl her brain was in, he'd lose interest. Fast.

"Yes." She'd have to do better than that!

But Todd didn't seem to mind. "I've seen you around. But you weren't at rehearsal this week."

So someone *had* noticed!

"I thought I was too far behind to catch up."

"Nah. Lots of people were missing this week. There were swimming competitions, and half the group either went to swim or to watch. Just come back on Monday. You'll be right along with the rest of us."

Then, much to her surprise, he touched the silver locket she wore on the chain around her neck. "Nice. It looks old."

"It is." She was inordinately pleased that he'd noticed it. "I found it in my grandmother's jewelry box."

Todd only smiled.

"Do you like to sing?" Lexi inquired, remembering Jerry's disinterested answer.

"Yeah, I guess I do. As long as it doesn't interfere with my swimming. Or my golf. Or basketball. Or . . ."

They laughed together. It was easy to laugh and be relaxed with Todd. He didn't have that preening, self-conscious air about him that Jerry had. He was comfortable inside his own skin—greasy as it might be at the moment.

"I suppose I'm interrupting your supper," Todd commented after calling his brother. "I can go and wait on the steps for Michael to pick me up."

"Have you eaten?" Lexi ventured, surprised by her own boldness.

"No. I seem to forget time when I'm under the hood of a car."

"I made some tuna salad and cut up a bowl of fruit. Would you like to join me? My family won't be back until after seven." Lexi's throat constricted at the end of the sentence. If he said no, she'd feel like a real dummy. And if he said yes, well, she might then too.

"I'd like that, Lexi. Thanks for asking."

She exhaled, not realizing until that moment that she'd been holding her breath. "Do you like lemonade?"

"I like lemonade a lot."

Her heart was beating so hard that she was afraid he could see it pounding through the thin cotton of her jumpsuit. She'd have to get a grip on herself if she were going to get through this meal intact. It pleased her that when she bowed her head for a silent grace, Todd did the same. Perhaps they had even *more* in common than she'd first hoped.

They sat on the redwood deck, eating and talking about Lexi's old home. When the doorbell rang, Todd's eyes reflected the twinge of disappointment she felt.

"That must be my brother Mike. He's *never* on time—until today. And for once he could have been late." Todd grinned, letting Lexi deduce what she would from that statement. "Thanks for supper. Next time, treat's on me."

She waved from the porch as Todd and Mike pulled away in the tow truck. Once it was out of sight, Lexi clutched her middle in an excited squeeze and did a dance around the porch. For the first time since her family's move, she was genuinely happy to be in Cedar River.

The following Monday, Lexi returned to rehearsal. She was disappointed to discover that Todd Winston was absent.

"Welcome back, everyone," Mrs. Waverly greeted the group, her beige hair bobbing and her glasses sitting low on her nose. "Because of the number of absences at rehearsals, I've made a change. I'm moving our performance dates from July to the middle of August. Publicity brochures will be going out next week. I expect you all to be here from now on. Otherwise we'll never be ready to perform—"

There was an audible groan building from the far corner of the room. Lexi could see Tressa and Minda spearheading the protest. Then Minda spoke. "But, Mrs. Waverly, summer will almost be over by then! You can't expect us to tie up our whole summer with—"

"You girls understood the responsibilities when you agreed to join the group. I don't believe there's any more to be said." Mrs. Waverly turned back to her music stand, as yet unaware of the mutiny that was brewing.

Lexi could see Minda and Tressa giving signals to girls throughout the rehearsal hall. Jennifer Golden muttered under her breath, "Oh, no! They wouldn't!"

But they did. In unison, every member of the Hi-Five, including girls Lexi hadn't realized were participants, like Gina Williams and Mary Beth Adamson, stood. Tressa spoke for the group.

"Seeing as it's summer and we don't *have* to be in this musical, we've decided *not* to be. Two weeks extra is more than we're willing to spend. As of right now, all Hi-Fivers have resigned from the summer cast." And without a backward look, Tressa and Minda led the girls from the room.

Jennifer's look was anguished. She loved to sing—belonging to Hi-Five had suddenly become very costly.

The room was vast and empty after the exodus. Many of the boys shuffled their feet uncomfortably. Jerry Randall was grinning in approval. He seemed to be the only one who thought the mass desertion had been amusing.

Lexi looked around at the girls who remained. All the flashy ones had left with Hi-Five. The sparrows were left. The canaries had walked out.

Mrs. Waverly seemed almost relieved. Her chin was set in a determined thrust. "Well, people . . . I guess it's up to us to prove that we can put together a musical without those voices. I'd like to hear you remaining girls sing the first few stanzas of the opening number. We're going to have to reassign some solo parts, and then we will continue as though nothing had happened. Bad behavior is not to be applauded. It is up to those of you who remained to prove that you are talented enough to carry the show. Are you up to it?"

Hesitantly, the girls began to nod. As they did,

the boys began to smile. There was new enthusiasm and purpose building within the group. Only Jerry didn't seem overjoyed with how little effect the walk-out had generated.

And best of all, these sparrows had a surprisingly sweet song.

Lexi missed Jennifer's strong, steady soprano. Other than that, it was amazing how little the other voices were missed. It quickly became obvious that most of those girls had not been putting their heart into the music from the beginning. And there were other benefits as well. Lexi was given Jennifer's duet—to be sung with Todd Winston.

"We're going to be working on your duet on Thursday and Friday," Mrs. Waverly instructed. "Todd will be back from his camping trip by then. The two of you may have to spend some extra practice time together to work it out."

So Todd was camping! Lexi wondered why he hadn't mentioned it on Saturday. But, then again, she didn't know him very well.

So pleased with her upcoming duet and enlarged roll in the musical, Lexi had nearly forgotten about the Hi-Five when Jennifer Golden called later the same day.

"Lexi! This is Jennifer. Congratulations! You did it!"

"What did you say?" Lexi had been at the piano all evening, fingering out the melodies to her new parts. She'd even chased Ben away when he had come with a box of blocks and begged to play.

"You did it! Don't you understand? You've been accepted by Hi-Five!"

"Oh."

"Is that all you can say? Lexi, this should be a big moment in your life!"

"I guess it is."

"Is something wrong? I thought you acted like you *wanted* to be a Hi-Fiver." Jennifer wheedled, surprised by Lexi's lack of enthusiasm.

"Well, I did. Until . . ." She hated to get into this with Jennifer.

"Until what?"

"Until you all walked out on the musical. That wasn't very smart."

There was a long silence at the other end of the line.

When Jennifer finally spoke, Lexi could hear the pain in her voice. "I had to do it."

"But you love to sing!"

"Mrs. Waverly was getting out of hand, Lexi. Dragging out the musical two more weeks! It's totally ridiculous! Summer will almost be over by then!"

"Would you *really* have minded if we had two more weeks to rehearse? I think we can use it."

"What are we talking about this for, anyway?" Jennifer parried. "You should be grinning from ear to ear. Tressa and Minda thought you were great!"

"I *am* pleased, Jennifer. Really. What happens next?"

"Nothing for a while. The other club members just get to know you. Then, when they feel like they know you well enough, they plan your initiation. That's when you're officially a member."

"Initiation?" Lexi didn't like the sound of that. It

sounded infantile and stupid—like having to wear a painted-on clown face and walk in old galoshes.

"Then you're really one of us. It'll be great, Lexi," Jennifer enthused.

"What was your initiation, Jennifer?" Lexi asked, curious. She wouldn't mind having a clue about what was in store for her.

The line was silent again. Finally Jennifer answered, "Oh, nothing much. We're not supposed to talk about it."

"What's the big secret?"

"It's just a rule Tressa and Minda have, that's all." Jennifer's voice sounded odd—empty—like she was talking through a hollow tunnel.

"Tressa and Minda seem to have a lot of power with this group," Lexi observed dryly.

"They're officers. They're supposed to make decisions. You should understand about that!"

"Don't get so defensive! I just don't remember anyone back home having that much power over anyone else."

"Well, you're not back home now. You'd better try to fit in with the kids here, or it will get awfully lonely."

Lexi bit her bottom lip. Perhaps Jennifer was right. This was a new place and a new time. And she'd had enough of lonely.

"And, Lexi . . ." Jennifer's voice had that odd sound again. "Don't bring your little brother up for a while. Just in case."

Lexi bit back her sharp retort. Why should her beautiful, lovable Ben bother anyone? She hardly heard Jennifer say goodbye. Finally the persistent drone of the line pierced her thoughts and she settled the receiver back into its cradle. The conflict that wrenched her apart every time she thought about Hi-Five tore at her again. Were these new friends going to be worth their price?

"Congratulations. I hear you got accepted into the 'inner sanctum' of Cedar River high society." Todd was smiling at her but his words sounded critical as they stood in the rehearsal hall at school.

Lexi's brow knit in a confused frown. Wasn't Todd Winston one of the boys that only a Hi-Fiver was good enough to date? The girls had said as much. They talked about boys a lot, and always insisted that whenever Todd decided to take a break from sports and antique cars, he would come to one of them.

But before she could analyze further, he continued. "I suppose we should get together to practice our duet. Any time especially bad for you?"

"No. All I really have is the musical this summer. I'm free most of the time." Lexi didn't mention her mysterious upcoming initiation or the fact that Ben had been terribly disappointed when she left today. Todd didn't seem all that enthused about news of Hi-Five, and she remembered too vividly what had happened to Jerry Randall's friendliness when he learned about Ben.

These days Ben was as miserable as Lexi could ever remember him being. Bored, restless, and uncharacteristically cranky, he was more and more demanding of her time—just as she was beginning to fill it with outside activities.

Fortunately, her parents had discovered a Little League team for the mentally handicapped that met every morning during the summer. Ben had attended for the first time today—and had come home happier than he had been in weeks.

She recalled their conversation.

"Well, Benjamin, how was Little League?"

"Fun!" He made swinging and pitching motions with his arms.

"Did you meet some new friends?"

"Friends."

"What position did you play, Ben? Were you the pitcher or the catcher?"

"Ben's a hitter! Attaboy, Ben!"

Lexi had smiled. Someone was encouraging Ben, she knew by the words he was parroting. Then her mind turned back to Todd.

"Why don't you set up a time to practice. What do you have to work around?"

"Swim team, my part-time job at the garage, the softball team I coach, and the hours I work for my mother. That gives us from six to seven A.M. and the hours between ten and midnight." Todd raked his fingers through his hair. "Maybe I've committed myself to too many things this summer."

No wonder he didn't date much! It was amazing that he had time to eat and sleep.

"My voice isn't very good in the morning, but if six is the only time, I can make it."

Todd's laughter rumbled from his chest in a wonderful chuckle. "Now, that's what I call a good sport! Let's just say I work two or three less hours at the garage for the next couple weeks. If we still need more practice, *then* I'll get you up at six A.M.!"

"Sounds fair. Where do you want to practice?"

"Either here at the rehearsal hall or, if you want, we could go to your house. It doesn't matter to me." Todd shrugged carelessly. "You pick."

Her house. Ben. Lexi desperately wanted Todd to come to her home, to meet her family, to spend time in her territory. But the memory of her experience with Jerry Randall still stung too sharply.

"The rehearsal hall has a better piano," she stammered. "Ours hasn't been tuned since the move. Maybe we'd better start out there."

Todd nodded in agreement. "Fine. Meet you tomorrow at four. If I'm late, just hang around. Mike always has just one more thing for me to do before I can leave the shop." He chucked her gently under the chin with his knuckles. Lexi could smell soap and a pleasant, masculine shaving lotion. His smile stayed with her long after he'd sauntered away.

Lexi's head was still spinning from the gentle touch when she heard the commotion behind her.

"Whooeee! Good going, Leighton!" Tressa sidled up beside her with a knowing grin. Apparently she'd come to check out the status of the musical without her and her friends.

"I'll say! Who'd ever have thought that our newest Hi-Fiver would be the one to shake Todd Winston off his high horse!" Mary Beth crowed. "We didn't make a mistake this time!"

Even Jennifer had a stupid smirk on her face. Lexi smiled grimly in response. These girls certainly took credit for everything a person did once she was a club member. That would take some getting used to.

There were a lot of things about Hi-Five that Lexi was having trouble getting used to.

"Lexi, Ben and I are going to the store. Do you want anything?" Mrs. Leighton inquired as she pulled a cotton shirt over Ben's head. "Shampoo? Toothpaste? Paper?"

"I do need some things for my costume for the musical. Maybe I should go along and pick them out."

"Fine. We won't be gone long. I promised your dad an early lunch."

"Why isn't Ben at Little League today?" Lexi wondered aloud.

"It was cancelled. Over half the team went on a field trip. A group of organizers are planning an overnight camping trip for the kids, and they took the older ones on a one-day excursion to show them where they'll be staying."

"Can Ben go too?"

"I don't know much about it yet. He's never been away from home before, so I'm not going to push him. I think he'd enjoy it if he had a friend or two for moral support."

"Who says the retarded are so different?" Lexi murmured to herself.

Jennifer's warning about introducing Ben to the Hi-Five was something Lexi hadn't thought about in days. The girls were nice enough—friendly, willing to include her.

In fact, the Hi-Five was far from Lexi's mind as she and her mother and Ben shopped leisurely in the shopping center on the distant side of Cedar River.

Mrs. Leighton had settled Ben in a chair with a

crayon and coloring book while she tried on jeans. Lexi had strict instructions to keep an eye on him. Still mindful of their last shopping excursion, Lexi kept one eye and ear tuned to her brother while she sorted through the sundresses on a lengthy sales rack.

She was hidden from sight when Tressa and Minda came up to the other side of the rack and to Ben.

Ben, who considered no one a stranger, looked up from his coloring to say, "Hi!"

Lexi watched as the two girls spun around to stare at the handsome, almond-eyed child. Ben smiled his most endearing smile, which turned crooked on one side, giving him a funny, gleeful look.

Tressa and Minda stared back, unsmiling.

Lexi could hear them whispering between themselves.

"What's wrong with that kid, anyway?"

"Aw, you know how weird little kids are. He's not very old."

"But there's something wrong with his face. It's kind of flat and his eyes are slanty. Do you think he's a retard or something?"

"Maybe. Who cares? It's nobody we know."

"Well, I think it's disgusting. Why would anybody take a kid like that out in public?"

Ben's head was swiveling from Minda's face to Tressa's and back again. He followed enough of their conversation to know they were discussing him. Sensitive, intuitive Ben didn't like their tone. Lexi could see tears building in his eyes.

"Maybe they had to. Maybe they couldn't help it," Minda offered.

"Well, if there was a kid like that in my family, I sure wouldn't flaunt it. Yuk."

A wave of nausea flooded over Lexi. She took a step toward the pair. Forget Hi-Five. That was her brother they were talking about! Just then, Mrs. Leighton emerged from the dressing room in a snug fitting pair of jeans.

"Hi, Ben! How are you doing?" Mrs. Leighton smiled, brushing the mop of Ben's hair into order. Then she noticed the two girls standing nearby, staring. "Hello, girls."

"Ha-ha-hello," they stammered in unison and began to back away. They came so close to Lexi that she could have reached out and touched them. Silently, she watched them beat a quick retreat.

A sad smile crossed Lexi's features as she heard Minda announce to Tressa, "Well, that little boy sure has a pretty mother!"

Lexi stepped out from behind the rack of clothing.

"Did you see those girls who were standing next to Ben?"

She nodded dumbly.

Mrs. Leighton persisted. "Did they say something to Ben? He looks very unhappy."

"They were talking about him." Her own voice was flat and miserable. "One of them didn't think he should be brought out in public. I'm sure he didn't understand their words, but I think he got the gist of their meaning."

Mrs. Leighton's lips clamped into a tight line. "When are people ever going to learn? Their ignorance and their fears make them so thoughtless."

Lexi hung her head. When was *she* going to

learn? She herself had been trying to deny Ben's existence lately. Until she could accept it, she could hardly expect anyone else to. A hard knot was building inside her. If only she didn't fear for her place in Hi-Five!

Lexi wondered what had happened to the girl she had once been. She'd never been ashamed of what Ben was before. And she wasn't now. Not really. She'd been a leader—and now she was trying valiantly to be a follower to girls she didn't even respect. What she needed was one friend who truly understood. Then she wouldn't care what the rest thought.

Suddenly the proverbial light bulb went on in her brain.

"Mom! I have to get home! I still have some lines to learn before I meet Todd to rehearse."

"Todd, huh?" Marilyn smiled. "Sounds like you're making a pretty good friend as a result of this musical."

Lexi smiled to herself. One good friend. Maybe that was all she needed.

Chapter Four

"How did you learn all these lines so fast, Lexi?" Todd stared at her in amazement. "Weren't you the girl who was too far behind to catch up?"

"Motivated, I guess. I don't want to make a fool of myself now that I have a larger part in the production."

"Yeah. Well, I'm glad you're my new singing partner. It was crazy of those girls to walk out on Mrs. Waverly like that. No sense of responsibility or commitment. I was really disappointed in Tressa and Minda for ringleading that mess."

Lexi pretended less interest than she felt for Todd's opinions. "Oh?"

"They're sharp girls. All of the Hi-Fivers are. But they pull such irresponsible stunts sometimes." Then his face creased into a smile. "But I hear you've been asked to join them. Maybe you can talk some sense into those airheads."

"Maybe." Lexi felt torn. So Todd did like the Hi-

Five girls. She'd begun to wonder. But still sharp in Lexi's memory was that little scene with Tressa, Minda, and Ben.

Just as they completed their work, Todd commented, "You know, this might sound conceited, but I think I bring out the best in you."

"What?" Lexi turned, surprised, and found herself only inches from his face, looking into his eyes.

"Your voice. It's so soft when you sing alone, but when we sing together, you really belt it out. I think I bring out the best in you."

More than you know, Todd Winston. More than you know.

Aloud, Lexi retorted, "Hah! It's me that brings out the best in you!"

Todd threw back his head and laughed. "Or maybe a little of both. I want my mother to meet you sometime, Lexi. You two would like each other."

Lexi's eyes widened with surprise.

"She's the administrator of a government service organization. She looks all soft and feminine—just like you. And inside she's a powerhouse that can't be stopped. I think you're like that."

"And I think you're giving me more credit than I deserve," Lexi demurred. "You haven't seen me do very much."

"Nothing except learn the entire musical score in twenty-four hours. And impress the most-difficult-to-impress crowd in Cedar River." He glanced at his watch. "And manage to make me late for swimming and not regret it. I'd say you're special, Lexi Leighton." Todd clamped his music to his chest. "But I won't risk getting kicked off the swim team to argue about it. I'd better get going."

He made his way from the music room door and flipped off the lights. Lexi stayed close on his heels. As he swung into his '49 Ford, Todd turned back.

"Too bad I'm all booked up for the weekend. Otherwise we could spend some time on this music. Maybe we can find a time on Monday. See ya, Lexi."

She watched his broad back disappear down the street, her disappointment so great she could almost taste it.

All booked up for the weekend. Probably with some Hi-Fiver she hadn't even met yet. Her hopes dashed, Lexi trudged homeward. Her own weekend loomed large and long before her. At least she had Jennifer Golden and the others to help occupy the time she had hoped Todd would offer to fill.

"Lexi! Thank goodness you're home! Will you take Ben outside and get him out from underfoot?" Mrs. Leighton looked more harried than Lexi could ever remember seeing her.

"What's he been doing, Mom?"

"Hanging on my leg, begging me to play. I don't mind playing with him, but I bought a lug of peaches at the store and started making jam. I've got boiling water and hot jars and everything dangerous for a curious moppet like Ben. He needs some outside entertainment."

"Don't we all," Lexi murmured as she went to find her brother. He was sitting forlornly under a birch tree, his hands jammed deep in his pockets.

"Hi, Ben. Whatcha doing?"

She was greeted with silence.

"Aren't you talking today, Ben?"

He shook his head mournfully from side to side.

"Do you want to play a game with me?" Lexi persisted, surprised by Ben's depressed behavior.

Ben shrugged his shoulders.

"What's wrong, Punkin?" Lexi resorted to her pet name for Ben.

Two tears rolled dejectedly down his cheeks.

"Come to Lexi."

She held out her hands and, suddenly wailing, Ben catapulted into her arms.

Lexi stroked his soft hair and crooned comforting, meaningless words. When the storm subsided, she held him away from her at arms' length and with mock sternness demanded, "All right, Benjamin Leighton, you tell your big sister what's going on. What made you cry."

"Lexi." Ben snuffled as he answered.

"What did you say?" Lexi was sure she'd heard wrong.

"Lexi made Ben cry." His distinctive features convulsed again and more tears threatened to spill.

"You'd better explain yourself, Punkin," Lexi muttered. Her stomach had tightened into an unpleasant knot. She hadn't been around all afternoon. How could she have made Ben so miserable?

"Sister's gone. Sister can't play. Sister's big girl now." Ben's voice had a sing-song, repetitive tone.

Now she understood. Lexi could hear her mother saying every one of those things to Ben in the course of the afternoon. It had all added up to "Lexi's deserted you, Ben" in his mind. Explanations would never do for Ben, only action.

"I'm here now, Ben. And I want to play with you. What games do you want to play?"

Lexi wished all of her problems could be solved so easily. Sunlight chased the storm clouds from Ben's features. The tears glistening on his cheeks were the only reminders of the sad little scene of moments before.

"Games! Play games!"

"What kind? Hide and seek? Kickball? Catch?" Lexi stood and pulled Ben to his feet.

"Catch! Catch! Play catch!" Ben went racing toward the garage for a ball. They played catch, kickball and hide and seek until Mrs. Leighton's jam was a row of crystal jars cooling on the ledge and the sun threatened to dip behind a cloud on the horizon. Then, holding hands, they went in to supper and an early night's sleep.

"Wake up, sleepyhead! We've got a big day planned!" Tressa's voice broke through the fog of slumber still hovering around Lexi.

"It's barely eight-thirty on a Saturday morning! Why are you even up yet?" Lexi groaned into the phone.

"Up? Minda, Jennifer and I never got to bed! We had a sleep-over trying to decide on your initiation."

"So what's it going to be?" Lexi cared little at this time of morning, but now that she was awake, she might as well know.

"We haven't come to an agreement yet. You'll know when we know. But that's not why I called. Want to go shopping?"

"I suppose. What time?"

"We'll be over in an hour. Jennifer needs a dress for a family reunion. With the three of us to help her, she can't lose. Bye!"

Lexi rolled her eyes upward. Whatever Tressa might be lacking, it wasn't confidence.

"Lexi play?" Ben asked over a bowl of snapping cereal. He spooned in a mouthful while he waited for her answer.

"Not today, Ben. I'm going shopping."

The disappointed droop to his shoulders told her more than she wanted to know. Lexi's mother came to her rescue.

"Ben, Daddy and I will play with you today. Do you want to go to the swimming pool?"

"Swim! Swim!" Ben began making fishy motions over his cereal.

"Thanks, Mom," Lexi breathed.

"It's difficult being the center of someone's universe, isn't it, Lexi?"

Lexi thought about what her mother had said as she dressed to go shopping. What would it be like to be the center of the universe for someone her own age? Like Todd Winston, for instance. She almost laughed aloud at the thought. Todd was so busy with sports and cars and jobs and the musical that he didn't need her cluttering up his life.

If he'd really thought she was special, he would have found a way to fit her into his weekend. As it was, she was grateful to the Hi-Five for giving her something to do this Saturday.

Lexi's gratitude turned to something more like irritation before the end of the day.

Shopping with Tressa, Minda and Jennifer took more patience than shopping with Ben. He, at least, had a reason for acting childish. After all, Ben was only eight.

It had begun at the perfume counter.

"Minda, if you spray one more kind of perfume on me, I'm going to be sick." Lexi waved the girl and the tester of perfume away.

"But this is advertised in all the magazines. I want to smell it."

"So try it on yourself."

"And smell like a flowerbed? No thanks. Come on, Lexi, be a sport."

This was not Lexi's idea of sporting. Neither were the hours spent in the shoe department trying on shoes that none of the girls intended to buy. Lexi sat disapprovingly by as the three giggled and wobbled in shoes intended for ladies twice their age. It was she who apologized as the foursome drifted off, leaving piles of shoe boxes in their wake.

"Let's go have lunch," Lexi pleaded. Her head hurt. The girls' high-pitched giggles were generating more decibels than her ears could stand. She was beginning to miss Ben.

"Look at this!" Minda whispered, pointing to a pile of silver coins on the lunchroom table. "There must be five dollars in change here. That's an awfully big tip."

"Maybe they ate a lot of food," Jennifer offered. "What are you doing?"

"Just hiding the money behind the napkin holder. Now the waitress will think we're the ones leaving the tip. Smart, huh?" Minda smirked at her own cleverness.

Lexi put her fingers to her pounding temples. Perhaps lunch would help.

It did, until they were ready to leave and, from the corner of her eye, Lexi saw Minda lift several quarters from the pile of coins on the table. Furtively, Minda slipped the money into her jeans' pocket and glanced away. Their eyes met and Lexi read the dare in the other girl's look. It was as obvious as if Minda had spoken aloud. *I dare you to tell the others what you just saw. If you do I'll ruin things for you in Hi-Five.*

Lexi dropped her eyes to the floor. When she lifted them, she saw the satisfied smirk on Minda's face.

Lexi was the last to pay at the till. As the others meandered down the hall into the mall, she called, "Go on ahead, I'll catch up." When they were out of sight, she hurried back to their booth and threw her last two dollars onto the table. Then she ran from the restaurant and hurried to meet them.

"Why so serious, Lexi? Is something wrong?"

Lexi glanced up, startled. "Hi, Mrs. Waverly. I didn't even see you standing there. What are you doing in my neighborhood?" She'd left the girls only minutes before. Home was less than a block away.

"I have an old friend who lives near here." The older woman studied her through the glasses perched on the tip of her nose. "I believe you would have walked right on by without even seeing me if I hadn't spoken."

"Sorry." Lexi's mind had been full of the questions she'd asked herself so often lately.

"Is there anything I can do, Lexi?" Mrs. Waverly's

pale-green eyes were kind. "I'm a good listener if you ever need to talk."

Lexi stared at her in surprise. Would Mrs. Waverly understand? Could she?

"Thanks. I'm not sure there's anything that anyone can do."

"Moving blues?"

"Partly."

Mrs. Waverly nodded sagely. "It's difficult to start over in a new place. In your old home everyone knew and understood you and your family. Once you leave that nice safe haven, you have to begin to teach people who and what you are."

"That's true!" Lexi nodded in agreement. "That's it exactly. But what makes it hard is that sometimes you aren't even sure who you are anymore—or how you got that way." Her shoulders sagged. "Sometimes I wonder why God gives us so many hard things to cope with."

Mrs. Waverly was silent for a moment. When she spoke her words were soft and well chosen. "Are you sure it's God giving you these difficult things, Lexi? Maybe you're blaming Him for things He hasn't done."

"What do you mean?"

"This world is a pretty messy place, Lexi. There seem to be a lot of people suffering that shouldn't be. We like to blame God for that, but I'm not sure we should."

"Why?" Lexi moved a little closer, oblivious to the traffic passing them, unaware of anything but Mrs. Waverly's kind face.

"If I thought it was God who sent us all our problems, I'd feel more like hating Him than loving Him."

"Yeah. I know that feeling."

"Instead, I like to think that He's the one who is there for us when something does go wrong. Not as the cause of our troubles but as our reinforcement. Somebody who builds us up and helps us manage to go on in spite of what life has dealt us." Then Mrs. Waverly blushed. "I'm sorry, Lexi. I do sound like I've climbed up on a soapbox and begun to preach. It's just that you looked so . . . forlorn."

Lexi grinned. Forlorn. What an old-fashioned word. Just like Mrs. Waverly. Old-fashioned but right on target. Suddenly she felt much better.

"Thanks, Mrs. Waverly. I'm not so . . . discouraged . . . anymore."

Lexi was still smiling to herself when she reached the back porch, but it faded quickly as her mother met her at the screen door.

"That does it! We've got to enroll Ben in a program for the handicapped. He's got to have something to keep him busy this summer! We can't go on like this any longer!" Lexi's mother threw a dish towel across the back of the chair and slumped into its wicker seat.

She'd just put Ben down for a nap. His miserable, heart-wrenching sobs tore at Lexi's heart.

"He hasn't cried when I put him to bed since he was nine months old," Mrs. Leighton said. "Until now."

"Then why now, Mom?"

"The move. I'm busier than usual. Your dad is never home. Getting the clinic started is taking every minute of his time. You've got new friends. He's lost all his. The poor little guy is all mixed up. We've got to make him as busy as the rest of us. He's just feeling left out—deserted."

A pang of guilt shot through Lexi. She had been dodging Ben lately. Back in Grover's Point, she'd been more than willing to take Ben with her when she ran errands or went for a walk. Here, she'd been leaving him behind. She'd convinced herself she was protecting him from the likes of Tressa, Minda, and Jerry Randall. But was it Ben she was protecting— or herself?

"What about Little League?"

"I've found that there's a more involved program for the handicapped as well. There's a very good organization here. I met the woman in charge. She's a real powerhouse. She told me that during the summer there are organized classes, crafts, and even overnight camping for the kids. I'm going to check into it first thing tomorrow. I can hardly wait."

Lexi nodded at that. She could hardly wait for tomorrow herself. Todd would be at rehearsal.

By rehearsal time, Lexi's stomach was tied in excited knots. Todd and Jerry sauntered into the music room together. Lexi felt a twinge of disappointment. She'd avoided Jerry as much as possible since their disastrous afternoon.

Todd looked even more tan today. His hair was bleached to ivory in spots from his weekend outdoors. He must have felt Lexi watching him, because he looked up and caught her gaze with his blue eyes.

"Hi." He mouthed the word rather than voicing

it, but it was all it took to send Lexi's heart into high gear.

The musical was progressing nicely. After the Hi-Five walkout, the others had banded together in determined camaraderie. Lexi was relieved that she hadn't been a new Hi-Fiver when that took place. She might have thought she had to walk out too. Jennifer was still unhappy about having lost her part in the production.

Lexi, Todd and Mrs. Waverly were the last to leave after practice.

"How are you two doing on your duet?" Mrs. Waverly inquired. She was more relaxed since the girls had staged their walk-out. It was ironic, but Lexi was beginning to think they'd done everyone a favor with their childish behavior.

"Lexi has it memorized perfectly. It's up to me now," Todd joked.

"Then I'm not too worried. Unless, of course, you get yourself involved in any more projects or activities." Mrs. Waverly seemed to know a lot about Todd and it was obvious that she liked him.

"No. I've got more than I can handle already this summer. In fact," and Todd turned a meaningful look on Lexi, "I've got so much to attend to that I haven't got time for some of the things I'd like to do most."

Mrs. Waverly spoke right over the commotion Lexi's heart had set up.

"The musical isn't far away. Then you'll have some free time."

Lexi wasn't looking forward to the end of the musical. She liked Mrs. Waverly. It was a pleasure to sing for her. They seemed to be on the same wave length most of the time. Perhaps it was because she and Mrs. Waverly attended the same church that Lexi felt such a kinship. And there was another reason Lexi didn't want the musical to end—then she wouldn't have an excuse to see Todd every day of the week.

"I'd better be going. Do you want to practice here or are you leaving?" Mrs. Waverly asked.

"Is your piano tuned yet?" Todd asked, turning a questioning look at Lexi.

She knew that the piano was not so out of tune that they couldn't use it. She also knew that she would like nothing more than to have her mother meet Todd. Todd would like their big old house with its rambling porches. But she didn't know how Todd would react to Ben.

"Not yet. Mom said soon, though. I'll tell you when." The words felt like sawdust in her mouth. She wanted Todd to share every part of her life. But she didn't want the two boys she cared about most to frighten each other away.

"Let's stay here, then. I have an hour to practice. After swim team I have to help my mom unload the camper."

"Did you go camping this weekend?" Was that what had Todd so "tied up" he couldn't see her?

"Sort of." He didn't elaborate.

Lexi wondered how one "sort of" went camping. But she was so relieved to think that Todd hadn't had dates with any other girls that she put the thought from her mind. After all, the musical was fast approaching.

When their practice time was complete, Lexi and

Todd walked together from the auditorium.

"My brother Mike has been here, I see," Todd announced.

"How can you tell?" Lexi wondered, her eyes searching the empty street.

"I parked my car over there. Now it's gone. He said if he had time he'd come and pick it up. I asked him to give it a good going-over for me. Mike's a great mechanic. He'll keep my old jalopy humming. By the way, do you have a ride home?"

"No, but that's all right. The exercise will do me good."

"We're only a couple of blocks from the garage. Mike's loaning me his motorcylce until he gets my car done. Walk over there with me to pick it up and I'll give you a ride home."

The thought of herself on the back of a motorcycle with Todd was just too delightful an image to pass up.

"Okay. Thanks."

Mike Winston's garage was a clutter of cars and teenage boys. Jerry Randall was at the center of the confusion. Lexi could see him putting the final buffing on his carefully polished vehicle. This was not the car she had ridden in on that ill-fated date.

She knew little about cars, but Lexi was sure this was an automobile meant for racing. Little painted fingers of flame were licking their way from beneath the wheel wells on the rear quarter panels. This was definitely not the Randall family car.

"On foot now, Winston? Did that old wreck give out on you already? I see it's back in the garage." Jerry's voice held a sneer.

Todd smiled. "It's just in for a checkup, Jerry. You know—maintenance."

"I'm sure you need lots of it when you insist on driving old junkers, Winston. You're lucky that your brother is a mechanic." Jerry buffed the fender of his car.

"I guess I am."

Lexi watched Todd from the corner of her eye. She could see the tenseness around his mouth and the disapproving manner in which he studied Jerry when Jerry wasn't looking. There was more going on between the two boys than she had first guessed. Todd was trying hard to hide his disapproval of Jerry and his showy car.

Mike's motorcycle was parked near the door of the garage. Todd brushed by Jerry and his friends to wheel the bike to the street. Lexi hung back, sensing that there was trouble brewing.

"So that's what you're driving, Winston! Why don't you get a horse?" Jerry crowed.

"This should take me as fast as I care to go, Randall," Todd said through clenched teeth.

"Then you must not care to go very fast, Winston. In fact," and Jerry paused as if studying the situation, "I wonder just how fast you can go. Care to find out?"

"I don't race, Jerry. I've told you that before."

"I must have forgotten how chicken you are about things like that, Todd. Too bad. It would have been fun."

Todd jerked his head, signaling Lexi onto the back of the bike. "Let's get out of here. When Randall gets in one of these moods, he's a real pain."

Todd handed her a helmet and she slipped it over her thick hair. This was Jerry at his most unpleasant. She didn't like what a fast car did to his ego. She wondered why she'd ever thought he was appealing.

Todd and Lexi roared away from the garage. An air tickle fluttered in Lexi's stomach. She liked the feel of the cool air on her arms and the fingers of wind touseling her hair. Her hands were wrapped cozily around Todd's middle. Her palms rested near his diaphragm and she felt, more than heard, him mutter a sharp word of frustration.

He was looking into the rear-view mirror. Tilting her head to do the same, Lexi saw Jerry's car edging up behind them, stirring up a cloud of dust.

Todd edged to the right of the road. Jerry's vehicle was coming upon them hard and fast. Lexi felt the muscles of Todd's stomach tighten. Something was wrong.

As Jerry's car neared, it seemed to edge closer and closer to the two on the motorbike. Lexi could hear the motor from beneath her helmet. Her mouth went dry with fear and she sent up a silent prayer for help.

Todd swerved, the wheels of the bike hitting the shoulder of the road. It took all his strength to keep the cycle upright on the shifting gravel. Lexi closed her eyes, sure they were going to meet the hard-packed road face first.

Instead, Todd brought the motorcycle to a halt. He ripped the helmet from his head and flung it to the ground. "Jerry Randall is a jerk! He's going to hurt somebody driving like that!"

Lexi struggled from the cycle, glad to be on solid

ground. "Does he do that often?"

"Jerry pulls one stupid stunt after another. It's like his brains turn to mush when he gets behind the wheel of that sports car. I've told him before that someday someone is going to be hurt."

Lexi was suddenly intensely grateful that it wasn't she or Todd who were Jerry's victims.

Todd looked at her apologetically. "I'm sorry. I'll try to get you home in one piece. Then I'm going to look up Jerry Randall and give him a piece of my mind."

"You aren't going to do anything . . . foolish, are you?"

"Like punch him?" Todd smiled grimly. "I've had the thought."

"Please don't get yourself in any trouble."

"Thanks for worrying. But you don't have to be concerned. Slugging Jerry Randall won't shape him up. I'm afraid nothing will. Nothing, that is, except an accident."

Silently, Lexi climbed back onto the bike. This move to Cedar River was bringing her more experiences than she'd ever imagined—not all pleasant.

Chapter Five

"Today's the day, Lexi!" Minda chattered. "Today you'll be initiated into the Hi-Five. Then you'll really be one of us. Aren't you excited?"

Lexi had expected to be excited. She really had. But other things had crept into her mind to distract her: Todd's "sort of" camping trip; Ben's unhappiness with their new home; the quarters Minda stole from the restaurant at the mall; her relationship with God, which she'd managed to push into the recesses of her mind; and Jerry Randall's behavior of last night. Those thoughts bumped around like skeletons in a closet. Only the realization that she would finally belong to a group consoled her. Lexi had been too active to enjoy sitting at home, waiting for school to begin.

"So, what do I do first?" Lexi joked weakly. "Put my clothes on backward?"

"That's kid stuff, Lexi! When you get initiated into Hi-Five, you have to really *prove* you're going to be a faithful member. Don't worry. We'll tell you what to do when the time is right."

Minda seemed to have it all figured out. She was obviously in charge of Lexi's initiation, a fact that made her very uncomfortable. Minda was the most flighty of all the girls in the club.

"Okay. I'll be waiting."

"Just meet us in front of the ice cream counter at Blanchard's Mall at two o'clock. See you then. Bye!"

Lexi stared into the receiver. Blanchard's Mall? What could they have planned for such a public place? If she had to walk down aisles singing or doing handstands, she was going to strangle the lot of them.

Her nerves didn't improve as the morning progressed.

Ben was up and gone before Lexi had finished clearing the breakfast table.

"Bye, Lexi!" He'd clung to his father's hand with one hand and waved with the other.

"Where are you going, Ben?" Lexi had inquired. "Aren't you leaving the house too early for Little League?"

"School!" he'd crowed. "School!"

"I've enrolled Ben in the summer program for the handicapped," Mrs. Leighton explained. "He has music and arts and crafts before his Little League game. I thought your dad had better get him settled in today."

"And we're going to be late," Mr. Leighton had announced. "Come on, Tiger, let's go conquer the world."

The last Lexi had heard of Ben was the roaring tiger sounds he'd made on his way to the family car. Maybe Ben felt as if he could conquer the world today, but *she* certainly didn't. She wanted to crawl back under her covers and hide. What *were* they going to do to her for initiation, anyway?

By noon Lexi was unable to eat her lunch.

"Lexi, are you sick?" Mrs. Leighton curled her long legs under her and gave her daughter a concerned look.

"No. Just nervous. Remember that Hi-Five club I've been talking about?"

"How could I forget? It's been the number-one topic of conversation for days!"

"Well, today is my initiation. And they won't tell me what it is. Apparently they do something different for everyone."

"Just something silly, I suppose. I remember when I was initiated into my sorority at college—"

"I don't think so, Mom. Minda Hannaford is in charge of mine and she . . ." Lexi paused.

"She what?"

"She can be pretty thoughtless."

"Just don't do anything that goes against your conscience or your Christian witness. There's no club in existence worth that."

"But—" Lexi started to protest.

"I know it's been lonesome for you here, Lexi. Your dad and I thought long and hard about how this move would affect you and Ben. Sixteen years in one place makes it difficult to leave. But you'll be fine. Don't compromise who and what you are for other people." Then Mrs. Leighton brushed away her serious comments with a sweep of one finely manicured hand. "I'm philosophizing when there's no need. I know what a strong faith you have. Go get ready for your initiation. You're probably going to have to eat a twenty-three scoop ice cream cone."

Later, Lexi was to wish it was as simple as that.

Minda, Tressa, Jennifer, and three other Hi-Fivers were waiting at the tables in front of the ice cream counter when Lexi arrived. Minda seemed more excited than usual and Jennifer, more subdued. Lexi tried to catch Jennifer's eye, but the blond girl dodged her look, hiding her expression behind her lashes.

"Here she is!" Tressa announced unnecessarily. Even she looked a bit anxious.

"Here I am," Lexi echoed. "Now what?"

"Mindy is in charge of your initiation, Lexi," Tressa explained. "We have every new member do something different to prove her loyalty to the Hi-Five. It was Minda's turn to choose an initiation."

Lexi chewed nervously on her bottom lip. She didn't like the odd glint in Minda's eyes—she was *too* excited by this. The others seemed to sense this as well. None of them would look Lexi directly in the eye. Jennifer appeared blatantly worried.

"Okay. So what do I do?" Lexi wanted this over with—quickly.

"Sit down and I'll tell you." Minda motioned to the molded plastic chairs. She lowered her voice so that the girls had to lean forward to listen. "I've thought about this for several days. Lexi, in order to prove her loyalty to Hi-Five, has to go into Grantling's Department Store and bring us back one item. Any item."

"Well, that doesn't sound so hard," Lexi breathed.

She tucked her shoulder purse under her arm and started to rise.

"You don't understand, Lexi. You don't get to take any money into the store." Minda had a painful grip on Lexi's arm.

Lexi sank back into her chair. "You mean *steal* something?" Her words came out louder than she had intended, and Minda clamped a silencing hand across Lexi's mouth.

"It doesn't have to be big, Lexi. A spoon or a spool of thread. Kids do it all the time," Minda assured her, as if her request was not the least bit unusual. "We'll be right here, waiting for you."

Minda gave her a shove and Lexi realized she was standing. Turning back, her eyes caught Jennifer's anguished gaze. Stumbling, she made her way to the front of the department store and slipped around the arched opening into the men's wear department. She needed to think.

She wouldn't steal. Not for anyone. Hadn't Minda heard of the Ten Commandments? "Thou shalt not steal." It couldn't be any plainer than that. There was no way she'd steal something—even if it meant she'd never have another friend in Cedar River.

"May I help you?" A pleasant looking young man in a suit was peering into her face.

"Could I sit down for a minute? I don't feel very well." Lexi's head was spinning with the possibilities—and she *did* feel sick.

The clerk offered her a chair near the dressing-room mirrors. Lexi sank into the vinyl seat and stared at her reflection.

What had happened to her, anyway? Where was

spunky, out-spoken Lexi? No one would have *dared* ask this of her back home! They all know about her beliefs, her values, her faith. They knew Lexi Leighton would never even consider stealing.

But that was the problem, wasn't it? No one knew her well here. She'd kept so many important facets of herself secret that she hadn't really allowed people to know her at all. She hadn't talked about her Christian faith. Why, most people didn't even know about Ben.

When the room stopped spinning, Lexi stood. Straightening her back and jutting her chin forward, she marched out of the store and back to the waiting girls at the ice cream parlor.

Jennifer's eyes were wide with wonder when she returned. She obviously disapproved of the stunt Minda had asked Lexi to pull, but wasn't brave enough to protest. The other girls were laughing and drinking sodas, seemingly oblivious to the dishonest act they'd asked her to perform.

"She's back!" someone whispered.

"Did you get it?" Minda held out a hand. She seemed surprised that Lexi had returned so quickly.

"I got it all right," Lexi announced flatly.

"What? What did you get?"

"I got my common sense back. If any of you think that I'm going to walk into a store and steal something just to be a part of your club, you're all crazy. You have no right to ask me to do something illegal. I'm a Christian, Minda. I can't do it. I *won't* do it."

Lexi stood rigidly before them, fury holding her upright even as her knees trembled with nervousness. Only the look in Jennifer's eyes rewarded her.

"You won't do it?" Minda hissed. Her slim face contorted in anger. "No one ever refuses!"

"Ah, Minda," Tressa interrupted, "maybe we did go too far this time. We'll just have to think of another initiation for Lexi."

"Yeah," Jennifer added, "that was harder than anything I had to do!"

Minda's angry eyes darted between Lexi and Tressa. Then the anger faded and a new emotion took its place. Lexi quickly decided she felt more at ease with Minda's anger.

"I've already thought of it," Minda announced.

"What is it?" Tressa inquired.

"It's not illegal or immoral or even silly. It will just prove that Hi-Five means more to Lexi than anything else. Do you guys approve?"

"We want to know what it is first, Minda!" one of the girls insisted.

"But it's my turn to do an initiation. You *said* I could do what I wanted," Minda protested.

Tressa weakened. "We did, you know. Are you *sure* it's nothing anyone could get into trouble for?"

"Positive."

"Well, then, it can be Lexi's initiation. Go ahead, Minda." Tressa's voice told Lexi that being president of Hi-Five wasn't always an easy job—not with Minda as a co-officer.

"To prove that she will be faithful to the Hi-Five, Lexi will have to quit the musical."

"What?"

"The rest of the group walked out days ago. If you'd been a member, you would have left then. I think it's only right that you prove your loyalty by leaving now."

The others, except Jennifer, finally nodded. The way Minda said it made it sound almost fair. But Minda had picked the only bright spot in Lexi's day and wanted to erase it.

"But I have a big part!" Lexi pointed out, her voice betraying the sudden panic she was feeling.

"You have Jennifer's old part. She left it. So can you," Minda announced with irrefutable logic.

Todd. The musical was the only time in a day she was sure to see Todd. *And Mrs. Waverly.* That poor woman had been forced to reorganize once because of Hi-Five. There weren't that many strong female voices left in the group. And Mrs. Waverly had been a good friend—one she didn't want to disappoint. At this late date Mrs. Waverly would have a terrible time finding a replacement.

And did she want to be replaced? No way. She squared her shoulders and stood tall. She was about to assert herself and it felt wonderful. Finally, the old Lexi Leighton—the one she was afraid had been left behind in the move—was back.

"No."

"Are you saying no again?" Minda's voice crackled with disbelief. The look in her eyes sent a chill skittering down Lexi's spine, but it didn't matter anymore. She'd finally remembered who and what she was—more than just the lonely new girl in town.

"I am. You're asking too much. I won't disappoint Mrs. Waverly and I won't disappoint myself."

"Then I don't think you're Hi-Five material, Lexi," Minda warned. The other girls squirmed uncomfortably in their seats.

"I'm sure you're right," Lexi murmured softly. "I don't know what made me think I was. Just lonesome, I guess. I'm only sorry it took me so long to realize how stupid I've been. But I'll have to find friends who understand me, who won't ask me to do stupid or unpleasant things."

"Don't count on it, Lexi. If you're not a Hi-Fiver, you're not anybody," Minda sneered.

"Then I'm proud to be a 'nobody,' Minda. I'll find some other 'nobodys' just like myself and we'll be friendly instead of stuck-up." Lexi gave a toss of her long hair. "I think it's time for me to leave."

Feeling as shaky as a wind chime in a storm, Lexi marched away from the cluster of girls, her head held high. She was as alone as the first day her family had moved to Cedar River. Only one thing was different. This time she felt good about it.

When Lexi walked into rehearsal that afternoon, she found herself the center of attention. Everyone in the room began to clap. Startled, Lexi paused, her eyes traveling across the smiling faces. Most of them were still strangers to her. The familiar ones, Todd's and Jerry's, were missing. One by one, the faces came to greet her.

"Thanks for not deserting us now. We'd never pull off the musical without your voice."

"Brave lady! I've never known anyone who stood up to the Hi-Five before."

People were pumping her hand in congratulations, and one girl threw her arms around Lexi and hugged her. It was as though she'd saved the musical single-handedly.

Mrs. Waverly was the last in line.

"I'm proud of you, Lexi. I know how difficult it must have been for you to refuse those girls. They're very persuasive. But the musical would have been ruined without you. You and Todd have something special together that I know I couldn't recapture with another voice."

Something special. Lexi would tuck that away to savor later. Right now she needed to know how everyone had found out. Surely Jennifer couldn't have talked to all these people!

"Mrs. Waverly, how did you find out I refused to join Hi-Five because of the musical? It just happened this morning."

"Your friend Jennifer Golden called me. She's been checking in with me every once in a while since she quit the musical. She wanted me to know that she was sorry about the situation. She was afraid the Hi-Five girls would make her leave the club since she was the newest member. But Jennifer loves to sing. She didn't want this to jeopardize any upcoming performances. I told her not to put up with their nonsense, but she's afraid. She isn't brave like you."

Brave! Lexi felt anything but brave. She'd just been mad. Those girls had nearly ruined her life.

Before Lexi could ask any more questions, Mrs. Waverly tapped her baton on the music stand. Rehearsal was about to start.

Todd and Jerry sauntered in just as they began the first song. Lexi wondered if Todd knew about this morning's episode, too. Would it change the way he looked at her?

After practice, Lexi pretended to be busy with her music until most of the group had filed out. But Jerry and Todd were still putting music stands away when she started to leave.

Jerry's voice trapped her at the door. "I hear you made the Hi-Five pretty mad today." He sounded amused. "That was a stupid thing to do."

Lexi spun around. "I'll be the judge of that."

"Okay, but I think you're nuts. You've got some strikes against you already—if you know what I mean. Making the most popular girls in town mad at you is a dumb thing to do." He shrugged lightly and brushed past her out the door.

Furious, Lexi stood at the entry, clutching and unclutching her fists. She wasn't even thinking of the Hi-Five. They weren't worth bothering about any-more. It was Jerry's sly insult to Ben that had her seething. How had she ever thought that she and Jerry could be a couple? She must have left her brain behind in the move. She was glad to have it back.

"I think you'd better explain what's been going on." Todd looked puzzled. He'd overhead Jerry but obviously didn't know what had transpired this morning. Thank goodness word hadn't gotten around to the softball teams already!

Todd took her by the elbow and steered her to-ward the parking lot. Lexi's sandal-shod feet fol-lowed his strong lead. When they came to the vintage car, he opened the door and motioned her inside. Lexi sank back on the cloth cushions, her head feeling too heavy for her neck to support. She hardly felt the car spring to life or pull from the parking lot.

She opened her eyes when the motor sputtered to

a halt. They were parked under an arch of trees. A pond lay before them, smooth as a mirror. Only the very tops of the trees moved, making sounds like the rustle of crinoline petticoats at a prom.

"Well? Are you going to tell me?" he prompted.

She rubbed her eyes with balled fists. "You must be the only one in town who hasn't heard."

"Softball practice isn't where I pick up my information," Todd agreed. "*You* are. What's been going on?"

"I refused my initiation into the Hi-Five this morning. Mrs. Waverly thinks I'm a saint and Jerry Randall thinks I'm a fool. I don't know which I am."

"Neither, thank goodness," Todd grinned. "How did it happen?"

"We met at Blanchard's Mall. Minda was in charge of my initiation."

Todd whistled through his teeth. "I can recognize trouble already. Minda has the common sense of a gnat."

"They wanted me to steal something from Grantling's Department Store. They shoved me off and I sat in the men's section wondering what to do next."

"Stealing! That's farther than I've ever heard of them going before." Todd's face was serious.

"Of course I couldn't do it. I'm ashamed that it went this far. Finally I went back and told them. At first, Minda was furious. Then she thought up a new initiation and she cheered right up."

"And what was that?" Todd sounded so concerned, so caring, Lexi wanted to cry. She was emotionally exhausted after this roller-coaster ride of a day.

"I was to quit the musical. All the other Hi-Fivers were out, so she said I should be, too."

"I've never given Minda enough credit for being devious," Todd commented dryly. "Her mind thinks in more convoluted patterns than I realized."

"I just couldn't do it, Todd! I thought about how disappointed Mrs. Waverly would be and how hard it would be to find a voice to fill in and our duet is almost perfect and—"

"And I'd refuse to sing with anyone but you." His voice held a smile. He'd captured a stray blond curl and wound it about his finger. "You saved the day, Lexi Leighton. I'm proud of you. Not everyone is brave enough to stand up to the devious tactics of the Hi-Five."

"But I thought you liked the girls in that club!"

"I do. Some of them. And some outside the club. I just like girls. Some more than others." Suddenly Lexi felt very warm inside. "Lexi?"

"Yes?"

"What did Jerry Randall mean when he said you've already got some strikes against you?"

She felt angry tears welling up in her eyes. Blast that conceited, egotistical, insensitive Jerry! She didn't want this moment ruined—because of Jerry or his crude innuendo about Ben. Just because he wasn't comfortable around a handicapped person, that didn't mean Todd would be uncomfortable too— or did it?

She wasn't going to honor Jerry's insinuations with an answer. Ben was too special to be dragged into this. She wanted to introduce Todd and Ben herself. She wanted Todd to know what a warm, loving little boy Ben was. Even with all the questions and confusion she'd had concerning Ben's handicap, mentioning him in the same breath as Jerry Randall just didn't seem fair.

"Who knows what Jerry means?" Lexi dodged. "He thinks I'm crazy to reject the Hi-Five."

"Didn't you go out with Jerry when you first moved to Cedar River?" Todd asked.

"We all make mistakes, Todd. Don't hold mine against me," she parried.

"I'm very proud of you, Lexi Leighton. You did the right thing today."

Lexi rested her head against the car seat. *The right thing*. She'd really goofed up this move. It felt good to be setting things right. Now if she could just do it where Ben was concerned.

But Todd's next words wiped even thoughts of Ben from her mind.

"You're more girl than Jerry Randall or the Hi-Five can handle, Lexi. I think I'll have to take you on as my special project. A friendship project. What do you think of that?"

"I love special projects."

Lexi and Todd sat watching the small, still pool. For the first time, Lexi felt at home in Cedar River.

Chapter Six

"Hi, Mom. Where's Ben?" Lexi padded into the kitchen on bare feet. The tile felt cool against her toes.

"He went with your dad this morning. He wanted to be at Camp Courage early. Because he started the program late, he was a project behind. His instructor thought it would be good for his self-esteem if Ben could catch up. Ben's going to go in a few minutes early and work on whatever it is they're doing. He says it's a surprise for the family." Mrs. Leighton's face beamed with pride.

Ben's accomplishments amazed Lexi. He'd changed from a frightened little boy into a confident youngster. He dressed himself each morning and waited patiently until one of his parents was ready to drive him to the summer program. His manual dexterity had shown improvement and so had his vocabulary.

"We're lucky there's such a good program for Ben in Cedar River. This move is turning out to be a real blessing for Ben."

Lexi nodded glumly. The tables had turned. It had been she who had been too busy to play with Ben after she was discovered by Hi-Five. Now, with those girls out of her life, Lexi had the time to play with Ben—and it was Ben who had no time for Lexi.

"But it's wearing him out, Mom. When he gets home he eats lunch and lies down for a nap. I hardly see him until suppertime!" she groused.

"Why, Lexi! I do believe you're complaining about Ben being too busy to spend time with you! Now, that's a switch. Two weeks ago it was the other way around."

Lexi hung her head. She'd begun to feel the repercussions of leaving Hi-Five. Her phone hadn't rung in days. Jerry Randall had worn an "I-told-you-so" look on his face all week. Todd's softball team was gearing up for tournaments and he was tied up every morning. His swim team practice had redoubled as well. Rehearsal for the musical was the only time she saw him.

But she wasn't sorry she'd quit. Only sorry she'd become involved in the first place. Lexi wasn't going to let loneliness force her into things she didn't want to do anymore. She'd learned her lesson the hard way.

"I'm going to tell Ben you've been missing him, Lexi," her mother added. "That will make his day. You're one of his best friends, you know."

One of his best friends. Lexi could remember being the *only*. She was glad he'd found a niche for himself. She'd driven him to it. But it was hard to share that adoration with anyone else.

That evening, Mrs. Leighton was as good as her word.

"Benjamin, do you know what happened today?"

Ben peered over his milk glass and shook his head. His shiny bangs swayed in a silken sheet.

"Lexi missed you."

His eyes grew big and his lips puckered into a silent *oh*.

"She woke up and you'd already gone to Camp Courage. She was looking for her best friend to play with."

"Friend." The silken locks began to dance as Ben nodded in understanding. "Lexi's looking for her friend—me!"

The family laughed. Ben's self-importance had taken two bounds forward with this conversation. When they quieted, Ben asked a question.

"Lexi lonesome?"

Suddenly everyone was silent.

Lexi felt tears spring to her eyes and rest precariously inside her lids, ready to spring out. Almost imperceptibly, she nodded.

Ben climbed down from his chair and, moving with his steady, distinctive gait, rounded the table to his sister. His hands gently ran across her face and down the tendrils of her hair. His almond eyes brimmed with compassion.

Lexi could almost see the wheels turning in his little mind. Still, she was amazed at the next words that came out. "Ben will fix. Ben will fix."

Touched beyond words, she scooped up her little brother and buried her nose in his hair. "You've fixed it already, Ben. Just knowing you care fixed Lexi already."

By the next afternoon, Lexi had forgotten Ben's promise to "fix" her loneliness. As a result, she was very surprised when Ben trudged around the corner of the house with a young redheaded girl in tow.

"Friend for Lexi, friend for Lexi," he sang, clutching the girl's hand and tugging her toward Lexi's perch on the deck.

Lexi jumped up and came running toward them, apologizing. "I'm sorry for my little brother's behavior. He doesn't understand. He's never done anything like this before. I hope he didn't scare you . . ." She stammered out excuses, hoping the girl wouldn't be offended, would understand.

"Oh, don't worry. Ben and I are buddies," the girl announced. "I met him the first day you moved in."

"You did?" Lexi gasped. She couldn't remember seeing this girl anywhere.

"Yes. Then my family went on vacation. We've been back a week. My name is Peggy, Peggy Madison." She stuck out a hand in greeting. "Actually I'm glad Ben dragged me into your yard today. I've been wanting to meet you."

"You have?" Lexi fought to keep the disbelief from her voice. "Why?"

"Mostly because I live right down the street. I was so excited when I heard you were moving in. I've always wanted a friend my own age on this block. You know, someone to walk to school and church and ball games with. And when I got back from vacation, I heard you were the local hero. I would never have dared just walk into your yard if it weren't for Ben."

"Local hero?" Lexi gasped. Whatever did Peggy mean by that?

"Don't you know?" Peggy seemed surprised. She tossed her head, throwing the thick mane of her hair back across her shoulder. She crinkled her short nose, wrinkling together the mass of freckles that danced across the bridge.

"Know what?" Lexi persisted, beginning to feel very odd.

"You've become the local folk hero among the girls in Cedar River. A role model. You stood up to the Hi-Five!"

"But I thought they were the role models around this town!"

"So did they." Peggy nodded sagely. " 'Movers and shakers' my dad calls them. But they managed to make anyone who wasn't a Hi-Five feel like a second-class citizen. Then you moved to town. Everyone just assumed you'd become a Hi-Five. Especially after Jerry Randall asked you out."

Lexi's eyes widened. Peggy certainly had a lot of information for having been gone most of the summer.

Peggy, seeing the look on Lexi's face, laughed. "Cedar River grapevine. Doesn't take long to catch up when you get back home." Then she continued. "When you refused to be initiated"—Peggy whistled through her teeth for emphasis—"you liberated us all, Lexi."

Laughter bubbled through Lexi, then at Peggy's theatrics. It felt wonderful to laugh—and have someone laughing with her. When the merriment subsided, Lexi choked, "Peggy, that's the craziest thing I've ever heard!"

"So I'm a little dramatic." Peggy had draped herself across a deck chair. The sun glinted through her red hair, making her look like she was on fire. "But no one ever questioned what those girls did until you came along. We let them walk all over us."

"I wish you'd been around to tell me all this weeks ago. It would have saved me a lot of time and trouble," Lexi commented.

"Oh, I wouldn't have dared!" Peggy gasped. "I saw you from the street the first day you came. You're so pretty and so confident! I couldn't have done that!"

Lexi smiled inwardly. Looks certainly were deceiving, she decided. But her old spark had finally returned. She'd defied Hi-Five.

"Well, enough about Hi-Five. Tell me about yourself." Lexi curled her legs beneath her and rested her chin on her knees. She had all afternoon to find out about her new friend, Peggy Madison.

"Aren't you girls *ever* going to come in off the deck?" Mrs. Leighton inquired. "You've had lunch out there and chatted away through Ben's nap. Is there anything left to say?"

Both Lexi and Peggy's eyes were shining. They'd discovered a hundred things they had in common—music, the ballet, a fondness for Agatha Christie mysteries, the ability to sew their own clothes, a passion for pralines and cream ice cream, and a mutual admiration for Todd Winston. They'd even be attending the same church.

"He's so nice, Lexi. I'm glad you're seeing him," Peggy enthused.

"That's generous of you," Lexi laughed, "but we're just friends."

"Still, I'd be insanely jealous if I didn't have a

perfectly nice boyfriend of my own. Actually, I'm surprised Todd's taken time out from his jobs and all the sports to see you. You must be pretty special."

"It sounds like I should be flattered. He doesn't say too much about himself. He's hardly mentioned that he has two jobs."

"He works for his brother and for his mom. He probably doesn't even think of it as employment. He just throws himself into whatever he does full force."

"Then he's a little like my brother Ben," Lexi smiled.

"Ben?"

"Uh huh. He's the reason you're here today, you know."

"Sure. I was outside your gate and he came toddling over, saying, 'Lexi's home. Lexi's home.' Next thing I knew he had me by the hand and I was meeting you."

"Ben thought I was lonesome and decided to help me out. And you know what? I'm glad he did." Lexi extended a hand.

Peggy grasped the outstretched fingers and gave them a squeeze. "Me too. That Ben knows what he's doing." Then she glanced at her wristwatch. "Yipes! I gotta go! See you tomorrow?"

Lexi nodded. "Call anytime." As she watched Peggy gallop across the yard toward her home, a smile softened her features.

A new friend. A nice friend. All because of Ben.

And Lexi's day was not over yet.

"Telephone, Lexi! I think it's Todd!" Marilyn called through the window. She muffled the receiver against the front of her blouse.

Lexi nearly knocked over the lawn furniture in her haste.

"Hello?" Her heart was thudding so hard she was afraid she wouldn't be able to hear his words.

"Hi! Busy?"

"No, not really. I met a new girl today. We spent the afternoon talking."

"Who's that? Anybody I know?"

"Peggy Madison."

"Nice girl. Her boyfriend Chad Allen and I are both on the swim team. The Allen family owns the big manufacturing plant on the edge of town. I'm glad to hear you found a new friend. Have you got plans now?"

"Not really. I was just going to—" She was about to say "play with my brother Ben" when she thought better of it. She needed to explain about Ben rather than just dropping him on Todd. "—help Mom with the housework," she finished lamely.

"Can it wait?"

"I guess so. Why?"

"My brother just called. He wants me to deliver a car for the repair shop. I thought you might like to ride along. Interested?"

Was she? Definitely! "Sure."

"Good. Be out front. I'll pick you up on the way to the shop. I'll be there in ten minutes. Bye."

That gave Lexi enough time to slip into white shorts and a rainbow striped top. She pulled her long hair into a ponytail wrapped with multi-hued ribbons.

She was waiting on the curb when Todd pulled into view. She'd given Ben a kiss on the top of his sand-covered head where he was playing in the back-yard. He was intently making his sandbox into a sand mountain. He'd hardly looked up to say good-bye.

"Hello, Rainbow! You look too nice to come near my brother's garage!" Todd leaned across the seat of his vintage car to open the door.

"You don't look like you're ready for it yourself," Lexi commented as she slipped inside.

He was dressed in pale blue and white. His white jeans crackled with newness. The powder blue and white striped shirt brought out his blond, surfer-like wholesomeness. His eyes darkened appreciatively as Lexi slid into the car next to him.

"My brother's going to be impressed."

He pulled away from the curb as Lexi settled against the scratchy-warm fabric of the seat. New cars were all plastic and vinyl. She liked the feel of the old-fashioned roughened cloth against her legs.

"This is a great car," she ventured.

"Yeah. I like it. It needs a paint job, though. I should have enough saved up by the end of the summer to pay for it. They don't make cars the way they used to."

They rumbled down the street. It was like riding in a tank compared to Jerry Randall's car. Lexi liked the solidness of the old car best. Solid. Like Todd. Unshakeable, steady, strong. They were traits she'd never appreciated before. She must be growing up, she decided. And, much to her good fortune, those qualities were nicely packaged in Todd.

Lexi found herself blushing at her train of thought. Todd would roar with laughter if he knew she was comparing him to his old car. Thankfully, the Winston garage came into sight.

They were met at the door by an older, dirtier but equally charming version of Todd.

"So this is Lexi!" Mike Winston grinned. His eyes crinkled at the corners just like Todd's, and his smile was as disarmingly even.

Suddenly Lexi felt very shy. Todd had told his brother about her! What had he said?

"Don't embarrass her, Mike," Todd chided. He put a comforting hand at the small of Lexi's back. "Just tell us where the car is and we'll take it out."

"It's the Mercedes over in the corner." Mike waved a wrench to his left. "Whatever you do, don't put a scratch on it. Don't even let dust land on it if you can help it! Melvin Hannaford is so fussy, he'd sue the socks off me."

Hannaford! That was Minda's last name. Could that beautiful machine be her father's car?

Todd read her mind. "Yup. That's Minda's dad. It's no wonder she's the way she is. Her dad's a real ogre sometimes." He turned back to his brother. "And how do we get home?"

Mike grinned and pulled a fistful of coins from his pocket. "Take the bus. I imagine you two can think of something to talk about in the backseat of a city bus."

Todd made a playful poke at his brother, who dodged it skillfully.

"Keys are in the ignition. Drive carefully."

"Are you going to be a mechanic, too?" Lexi wondered. "Like Mike?"

"Me?" Todd chuckled. "No thanks. I want to repair people, not cars."

"A doctor?"

"Sports medicine." He grinned. "I've already had enough sprains, tears and scratches to get a degree."

Halfway to the Hannaford home, Lexi began to get nervous. "What if Minda's home to accept the car, Todd?"

"What of it? It's her house and it's her dad's car."

"She's not going to be happy to see me."

"Then she'd better get used to it. School starts soon and she's going to see you every day—with me."

It *was* Minda who came to the door of the sprawling ranch house.

"What are you doing here?" were her words of greeting.

"I'm delivering your dad's car," Todd announced. "Here are the keys."

"Then, what's *she* doing here?" Minda sneered as she took the keys from Todd's hand.

"She's with me. Come on, Lexi." Todd took her by the elbow and steered her toward the arched gate through which they'd driven. "There's a bus due in about five minutes."

Lexi could feel Minda's eyes boring into her back all the way down the drive. She'd seen hatred in the girl's eyes. Hatred and something else. Fear?

Lexi was still shaking when they boarded the bus back to town.

"Don't let her get to you, Lexi. Minda's a spoiled brat."

"She hates me, Todd. You can just see it."

"You're the only one who's never given her exactly what she's wanted, that's all. She doesn't know how to control you and she doesn't like it."

"You seem to understand her pretty well."

Todd shrugged. "I've known Minda a long time."

"How well?" Lexi hated the questions her curiosity was making her ask.

"Do you mean, have I dated her? Yes. I have. But it didn't work out. She didn't like it when I worked at the garage. Said I smelled like gasoline all the time. And when I worked for my mom, well, she *despised* that. She wanted to control me and I didn't want to be controlled." Todd shrugged and added, "Ancient history, Lexi."

Lexi wanted to ask what kind of work Todd did for his mother, but the bus pulled up in front of Mike Winston's shop, cutting off their conversation.

As they climbed back into Todd's 1949 Ford coupe, he snapped his fingers with a loud crack. "Lexi! I'm sorry! I forgot to ask you!"

"Ask me? Ask me what?" Startled, she turned large brown eyes to his face.

"Do you want to watch my softball game tonight? It starts in less than an hour."

"Is this the team you coach?"

Todd laughed. "No, not quite. This is the one I play on."

"Then when do I get to see the team you coach?"

She watched his look soften, "Give me a couple more weeks with them and I think they'll be ready. I want them at their best. Otherwise they'll be shook when the coach brings his girlfriend."

The coach's girlfriend! Lexi felt tickly inside, just like her stomach had felt on the roller-coaster ride at Valley Fair.

"Last year I coached a girls' team. They would

have scratched your eyes out," Todd continued. "I was a pretty popular guy last season."

The tickly feeling was replaced by a twinge of jealousy. A girls' team?

"Well," he demanded, "are you going to watch my game tonight?"

"I'd love to. But I have to call my mom."

"Let's do it from the ballpark. I have to get changed and out on the field."

That was how Lexi found herself sitting front and center on a section of splintered bleachers cheering her heart out for the home team. And that was where Jennifer Golden found her, eating popcorn and keeping her eyes riveted on the handsome pitcher.

"Hello, Lexi." Jennifer's voice sounded far away and tentative.

"Jennifer! Hi. Would you like to sit down?" Lexi dusted off a spot on the bench next to herself.

"Thanks. I'd like that." Jennifer seemed at a loss for words. She planted herself heavily on the seat next to Lexi.

"Popcorn?" Lexi offered, not sure what to say or do. Though Jennifer had been the one to spread the word of her rejection of Hi-Five, she wasn't sure whether the girl approved of her actions or not. "Okay." They sat in silence. Finally, between innings, Jennifer spoke.

"How are you doing?"

"Just fine. How about you?"

"So-so."

"Is something wrong?" Lexi was concerned about Jennifer's subdued attitude. She was only a shadow of the girl Lexi had first known.

"Kind of."

"Want to talk about it?"

"I wish you were in Hi-Five, Lexi. Then I'd have someone I'd feel comfortable with in the club."

Lexi's eyebrows shot up in surprise. Apparently, even being a member of Hi-Five didn't guarantee friendship within the group. "I think I've ruined my chances of ever being a Hi-Fiver, Jennifer. Even if I wanted to be a member, which I don't. Sorry."

"I wish I'd never joined, Lexi. You don't know how smart you were to get out!" The words poured from Jennifer—about her unhappiness, about the disappointment she felt, about her desire to be in the upcoming musical.

"If you don't enjoy it, Jennifer, why don't you quit?"

"I'm not as brave as you are, Lexi. I don't want Minda angry with me."

"I'm not brave. I just came to my senses. And I don't care if Minda is angry or not. That's her problem, not mine."

"She might try to make it your problem, Lexi. Minda's like that."

Lexi remembered the hateful look Minda had showered on her when they delivered the car. She shrugged. "Then let her try."

"That's what I mean about you, Lexi. You don't worry about what other people think. I even let go of my part in the musical to go with those girls. And I really *cared* about that."

"You could still be in the musical, Jennifer."

The blond girl snorted in derision. "That's a laugh. It's only a week away."

"You could be in the chorus. You've got a powerful voice. I'll bet Mrs. Waverly would be glad to have you back. You could learn the music. After all, you know most of it from before the walkout."

Jennifer's eyes softened. "I guess I do. Do you think Mrs. Waverly would let me?"

"She knows you didn't approve of the walkout. But," and Lexi paused to emphasize her next words, "you'd have to quit Hi-Five. They'd never let you sing in the musical after all this trouble."

"I've thought about it. I miss you, Lexi. And Minda says none of us are supposed to have anything to do with you. Tressa and the others tried to disagree, but Minda has it in her head. She insists that as long as she's an officer, she makes the rules."

"Whatever happened to parliamentary procedure?" Lexi chuckled. She was more relieved than ever to be out of that clannish, nearsighted little group.

Jennifer grinned widely then, for the first time. And the pair settled back to watch the rest of Todd's game.

"I see you and Jennifer made up," Todd commented. He was still towel drying his hair as he came out of the locker room. He smelled like shampoo and newly applied shaving lotion.

"I don't think we were ever fighting. She was just scared to talk to me because of Minda."

"So it's Minda now, and not the entire Hi-Five?"

"I'm beginning to believe it's always been that way. In fact, Jennifer's considering coming back to the musical."

"Now? Isn't it too late?"

"Not to be in the chorus."

"Oh, that would be all right, I guess." Todd stopped and put his index finger under Lexi's chin. "But I'm not giving up my duet partner now. Remember that."

How could she forget?

Lexi was still smiling when they stopped at the Hamburger Shack on their way home. Jerry Randall was working in the back and several of the Hi-Five were at their customary table.

Lexi paused at the door. Todd, his hand at the small of her back, felt her hesitation and whispered, "Would you rather just go home?"

"No. I'm not going to let them chase me out of a public place. You'll protect me from the claws of Hi-Five, won't you?"

He smiled down at her. "Definitely."

Lexi led the way to a booth. She could feel several pairs of eyes boring into her. Minda's were the only ones shooting daggers.

Lexi, seated with her back to the group, forgot about them over hamburgers and malts.

It was not until Minda's voice assaulted her that she remembered the crowd was not altogether friendly.

"Well, look who's here! The traitor and her constant companion!"

Todd and Lexi stared at the girl in surprise. Apparently frustrated by her inability to get under Lexi's skin, she'd decided to include Todd in her barbs.

"I didn't think you'd start slumming like this, Todd. Really. I thought you had better taste in girls."

"I think my taste is getting better all the time, Minda." His voice was clipped with irritation.

Minda's face convulsed at the implied insult. Minda had been Todd's very first girlfriend, Lexi deduced.

"That was mean, Todd." Minda obviously couldn't take it as well as she could dish it out.

"So was your comment. I'll apologize for mine if you apologize for yours." Todd's arm rested lightly against the back of the booth. Lexi felt sick. She'd never meant for former friends to become enemies.

"But mine was true."

"Then perhaps mine was too."

"Todd, maybe we'd better leave." Lexi plucked at the sleeve of his shirt.

"Run on home, Miss Religious Prim and Proper. And take your pious boyfriend with you. It won't be long until he gets tired of a goody-two-shoes like you and drops you, too." Minda flipped her hair around her shoulders and sauntered back to her group. Only Lexi saw the hint of tears in the girl's eyes.

Todd and Lexi were quiet until they reached the car. Then Todd spoke. "Don't let her get to you, Lexi."

"But now she's attacking you, too!"

"I can take care of myself. I understand Minda."

"I wish I did." Her words came in a sigh.

"Minda doesn't have a very happy home life, Lexi. I've seen her dad slap her across the face for talking back. Her mom spends her days at the country club just to be away from Mr. Hannaford. I think Minda wants to have control somewhere, with somebody. She's picked Hi-Five. You're a threat to her. You won't be controlled. You have beliefs and you stick to them. Anyone with that much confidence scares her. You don't have to change. Just remember that it's Minda's problem, not yours."

"How'd you get so smart, Coach?"

"You should meet my mom. She taught me everything I know."

"I'd like that. I'd like you to meet my family too." Lexi thought of Ben.

"Maybe at the musical."

"Maybe," Lexi murmured as she slipped from Todd's car to the sidewalk in front of her house. "Just maybe."

"Benjamin Leighton, what are you doing out of bed this time of night?" Lexi blurted when she floated into the living room. The dreamy bubble Todd had created for her was burst by all the lights and confusion inside the house.

"Surprise! Surprise! Ben made a surprise!" He clapped his hands with unrestrained glee.

"We let him stay up to show you his project, Lexi. His day-camp instructor brought it over. He was too excited to sleep, anyway," Mr. Leighton explained.

"Well, what do you think?" Mrs. Leighton demanded.

Ben's project was a mural, painted on newsprint, spanning the length of the living room. He had painted, in vivid colors, his ideas of his family.

Ben had drawn himself, she could tell by the almond-shaped eyes on the smallest stickman. Then her parents appeared. They were standing in the oddly angled square that surely represented their house, holding hands. Then there was Lexi. Her figure was big as life and adorned with long blond hair, streaked with shades of purple.

"It's just beautiful, Ben!" Lexi gasped.

"Beoootifulll!" Ben cheered.

"But, Ben!" Lexi announced, studying the painting some more. "There's another person in this picture! There are only four of us. Who is this person you've painted?" Lexi pointed to the fifth stick person on the mural.

Ben marched to his creation and stuck out a short, stubby finger so characteristic of Down's children and announced, "Ben's best friend." Lexi and her parents all muffled sounds of surprise. It was the gentle family joke that Lexi and Ben were the best of friends. "All right, Benjamin! Tell me who this person is! Tell Lexi who took her place!" Lexi pulled Ben toward her and made a little dance around the room.

"Big fellow! Big fellow!" Ben reiterated. "Best friend! Big fellow!"

Marilyn laughed and uncurled from her perch on the chair. "This little fellow had better get to bed now that we've had the unveiling of the latest piece of Benjamin Leighton artwork. You can solve the mystery of Ben's new best friend in the morning, Lexi. You'll have to teach Ben to remember names."

Laughing, the Leighton family made their way to bed.

Chapter Seven

For the next week, the musical took all of Lexi's time and energy. She even forgot to inquire about Ben's mysterious new best friend. Guiltily, she thought about how little she'd involved herself in Ben's life this summer. She hadn't even watched him play in a Little League game.

"After the musical," she promised herself. "*Then* I'll go visit Ben at day camp."

"What are you muttering about?" Jennifer came up behind Lexi as she bent over a piece of backdrop scenery, painting a vase onto a one-dimensional fireplace.

"Ben. I haven't had a minute for him lately. Lucky for me he's found some new friends at Camp Courage."

"Camp Courage. That's quite a name." Jennifer squatted down beside her friend.

"It's a good one. Those handicapped kids have more courage than we can ever imagine."

"Why do you say that?"

"Just imagine how brave a handicapped child has

117

to be to walk across a floor in braces or with flawed coordination. Every minute he's got to accomplish something we take for granted." Lexi's voice grew soft. "I'll never forgot how Ben struggled to learn to walk. I prayed about every step he took. I would have made him give up if I could have. But he wouldn't. He'd just fall down, cry a little, and get up again."

"I guess I never thought about it that way." Jennifer's voice was hushed with new-found admiration. "And I thought *I* had it tough!"

Lexi turned to smile at her blond friend. "You were pretty brave to resign from Hi-Five, Jennifer. And then to make an appointment with Mrs. Waverly to see if she'd let you return to sing in the chorus!"

"I don't know which was worse—Minda or Mrs. Waverly. Minda, I think. She acted like a wild woman. All Mrs. Waverly did was give me a ten-minute lecture and scare me out of my wits before she agreed to let me come back!"

"I'm sorry Minda was so hard on you, Jennifer. I suppose part of that is because of me."

"*All* of it is because of you in Minda's mind. Her little world is crumbling and, the way she sees it, it's all your fault."

"What do you mean 'her little world is crumbling'?" Lexi daubed at the backdrop thoughtfully.

"Some of the girls—especially Gina and Mary Beth—didn't like the way she tried to handle your initiation. It embarrassed them, I guess. They'd never asked anyone to steal before. Some of them think that Minda went too far."

"I'm glad to hear that not everyone agreed with her tactics."

"But Minda blames *you* for her own bad judgment. She thinks that if you'd gone along with her, no one would have said any more about it. Now the girls have told her that she can't be in charge of an initiation again and she's *furious*." Jennifer emphasized her final word with a grimace.

"You and I don't have to have another thing to do with Minda until school starts. Maybe she will have cooled down by then," Lexi shrugged. She'd wasted too many hours worrying about Minda and her tantrums already.

"Don't count on it. Mrs. Waverly told me something that's going to toss us right back into the fire with Minda."

"What?" A bolt of alarm zinged around in Lexi's midsection. Another face-to-face with Minda was too much right now.

"Mrs. Waverly and the summer band instructor cooked up this 'wonderful' idea. They've been rehearsing some of the music we have. The band is going to play the overture and finale. They're going to be here for all the dress rehearsals as well as the performances. You can look out across the stage lights and see Minda glaring back at you from the flute section. What do you think of that?"

Lexi groaned. "Oh, no! How can Todd and I sing our duet with her under our noses?"

"You could give the duet back to me," Jennifer suggested slyly.

She laughed out loud when Lexi punched her in the arm. "No chance, Golden! That duet is mine! And"—Lexi paused to study her friend—"I'm grateful that you haven't held it against me because it was given to me."

Jennifer shrugged. "Better you than anyone else, Lexi. You and Todd have an electricity between you which will make that number the best in the show."

"Todd! I'm glad you mentioned him! I promised to deliver our costumes to the dry cleaners. I'd better hurry if they're going to be done in time." Lexi jumped to her feet. "Want to come along?"

"Sure. It's worth the walk just to get another look at those costumes. They're gorgeous."

"I know. They're the only ones on loan from the college theater department. Everyone else has to make do with last year's leftovers," Lexi said as they hurried toward the wardrobe room.

"You and Todd are going to make one spectacular couple up on stage, Lexi. I can hardly wait."

Neither could she, Lexi decided. As she walked home from the dry cleaners, she thought about the baby blue off-the-shoulder gown she'd just delivered. It had miles of petticoats and a delicate blue rose that decorated the bodice. She'd fit into the dress without any of the confining undergarments that gave the others who'd worn it the tiny waist. The color and style were exactly right.

And Todd's costume would complement it perfectly. He would wear a white tuxedo with a blue sash and shirt. He was to carry a cobalt-blue cane to balance the big southern-belle parasol she'd rest across her shoulder. When the lights went down and they came on stage in the circle of the spotlight, everything would be perfect.

Her pleasant thoughts were shattered as she reached the front gate of her home.

Minda stood on the sidewalk, scolding like an angry magpie. Ben hung on the inside of the gate, tears streaming down his face.

"What's going on here?" Lexi demanded, putting an arm across Ben's quivering shoulders.

"I was walking by and this little creep hit me with the gate."

"Ben wouldn't do that."

"Well, he did. I walked up to it and he was swinging on it and he hit me."

"It was an accident, then. Ben doesn't have very good coordination. He probably couldn't stop swinging in time." Lexi put an arm around Ben's trembling shoulders.

"Then he shouldn't be allowed out of the house. People like him shouldn't be allowed out anyway."

Lexi bit the inside of her cheek until she tasted the tang of her own blood. Counting to ten and praying she wouldn't scratch Minda's eyes out before she got there, Lexi demanded, "What are you doing here, Minda? If you hadn't been trying to get through the gate, none of this would have happened."

"I came to see if the rumors were true."

"What rumors?"

"That you had a retard for a brother." Minda stared clinically at Ben. "Guess it is true. Maybe that's why you act like you do. You're not all there either."

Lexi's mouth dropped open in astonishment. When she recovered, her tone was icy. "Get out of here."

"You can't be as smart as you think you are, Lexi Leighton," Minda persisted. "Look at your brother. Don't things like that run in families?"

"Now, get out! Now!" Lexi took a menacing step forward.

Finally Minda, who'd been so engrossed in her own hatred, saw the look in Lexi's eyes. She stumbled backward three steps before she turned and ran.

"Retard. Retard." Ben mimicked, his tears diminished now that Lexi was there.

"No, Ben. No!" Lexi attempted to clamp a restraining hand across Ben's mouth, but the tears flooding her eyes made him a watery blur.

"What's going on here?" Mrs. Leighton demanded as she hurried to the gate. Her hand still held the garden spade she'd been toiling with at the edge of the yard.

"Retard. Retard," Ben repeated.

"Lexi?" Her mother's voice held astonished concern.

Lexi poured out the entire story as her mother led Ben back to the house.

Inside, Mrs. Leighton poured generous glasses of lemonade and filled a plate with spice cookies, trying to soothe the distraught pair. When Ben's face was washed and he was settled with a puzzle and his snack, she turned to her daughter.

"This is something I've always worried about. I guess we've been lucky that nothing like this has happened before."

"What do you mean, Mom?"

"Insensitivity, lack of understanding, fear, cruelty. We've been lucky not to have encountered it before this. Not everyone understands the retarded, Lexi. Some people choose to ignore the reality of the handicapped; others are unthinkingly cruel."

"Minda was thinking, all right. And saying what she thought."

"But she wasn't thinking of Ben. She just assumed that he couldn't understand her. She was trying to hurt *you*, Lexi. Ben was just her tool."

"Well, she did it, then," Lexi acknowledged. "I *hate* her!" Then a new, bone-shuddering thought hit her. *And I hate God for doing this to Ben.*

"Returning her anger won't accomplish anything, Lexi. Remember what the Bible says about forgiveness." Mrs. Leighton's soft, logic soothed. "And you don't *really* hate her, do you?"

"No, I guess not. I just got so *mad*! She's blaming me because she's in trouble with the Hi-Five. Everything has turned around for her. I've got friends and she's losing hers."

"That's pretty hard on a teenage girl. Remember how miserable you were when we moved?"

Lexi nodded grudgingly. "But she shouldn't have done it!"

"Of course not. But we don't want to validate her ignorance and cruelty by responding the same way." Mrs. Leighton brushed a strand of hair from Lexi's forehead. "If more people understood the handicapped, there would be less thoughtless behavior."

Lexi nodded. "Jennifer said she didn't know how nice a kid like Ben could be. She said at first she thought he couldn't do anything for himself or even think for himself."

"We all know better than that, don't we? I'm proud to say I've raised two children who can think for themselves."

"Now that Jennifer knows him, she thinks Ben

is a neat little guy. But I don't think letting Minda get to know Ben would help her. I don't think anything could help her."

"We don't know very much about Minda's background, Lexi. Maybe no one has ever taught her to be sensitive to others."

"I know she's rich," Lexi observed, remembering the huge ranch house and the Mercedes.

Her mother chuckled. "Money can't buy common sense—or happiness. But don't think about Minda anymore today. You have to be the best person *you* can be, with God's help. That's a hard enough job without trying to change others. And Ben seems to have survived his ordeal pretty well."

Ben's dark head rested on his crossed arms. His eyes had drifted shut and his lips curled in a smile. As Lexi cleaned up the lemonade glasses, she wished that she could put Minda's behavior out of her mind as easily as Ben had.

"Get those backdrops to stand straight! We can't have the antebellum plantation tumbling on Lexi and Todd's heads!" Mrs. Waverly swung her baton with a fury. Tonight was the premier performance and the backdrop of New York City wasn't even completely dry.

"Next year I think she'll chose something less complicated than a variety musical," Todd whispered in Lexi's ear. "There must be plays on Broadway that require less work than this."

Lexi giggled and nodded. Mrs. Waverly's hair stuck out in clumps just like Ben's did when he awoke from his nap. She was thankful that most of her own work was done. All that was left now was to walk onto the stage with Todd tonight.

If she could avoid Minda with her flute and her glaring stares from the orchestra pit, she'd be home free.

"Did you pick up the costumes?" Todd asked as they strolled to the back of the stage.

"No. The dry cleaners promised to deliver them this morning. Didn't you see them in the back?"

"Let's go and check. I didn't see anything when I came in."

Lexi's stomach knotted as they headed for the dressing rooms. The cleaner had promised to take special care with the dress.

A uniformed delivery man was entering by the stage door. "Here's that suit for tonight. Where do you want me to hang it?" He had Todd's white tuxedo in his hand.

"But where's the dress?" Lexi asked.

"No dress, missy, just the tux."

"But I dropped off a dress at the same time as the tuxedo! It should be on the slip."

"Yep. Says right here, blue floor-length gown," the delivery man agreed.

"Then, where is it?" Todd pushed his way forward.

"It's crossed off—says 'picked up' next to it. Did you pick it up, missy?" The man looked at Lexi questioningly.

"No. No! I didn't! We've got to find that dress!" Panic filled Lexi's mind. Her beautiful dress! The romantic moment on stage with Todd! It would never be the same without the dress!

"I'll give you one guess who's got it," Todd commented.

Lexi's eyes flew open. "Minda!"

"I'd bet my '49 Ford on it. She's been lying low during rehearsal these past two days. Probably hoped no one would discover it was missing until tonight. Then she could enjoy the confusion she'd created."

"Why, Todd? Why is she doing this to me?"

"I think we'd better ask her." His voice was grim. "Jennifer! Have you seen Minda lately?"

Jennifer laughed humorlessly. "She hasn't been hanging around me, if that's what you mean. I saw her duck out about fifteen minutes ago."

"Let's go." Todd steered Lexi toward the parking lot and the '49 coupe. It seemed forever until they pulled into the Hannafords' yard. Todd had a determined set to his chin. Lexi was thankful he was on her side.

They found Minda on the cobblestone patio, drinking a Cola.

"What are you two doing here?" Minda jumped up, spilling the soda across the lawn table.

"We came for the dress."

"What dress?" she responded, but both Todd and Lexi had seen her hesitation.

"Lexi's costume for the musical tonight. You picked it up at the dry cleaners. It was supposed to be delivered."

"You can't prove it."

"I bet we can. Whoever waited on you can describe you. Maybe you even had to sign for the dress. Shouldn't be hard to prove, Minda. If you're so sure you didn't pick it up, then you won't mind coming with us to the dry cleaners while we ask him a few questions. Just to clear your name."

The other girl's resolve was weakening. "Get out of here. You don't have any right to be at my house. I didn't invite you. I—"

"Minda? Do you have company?" A taller, older version of Minda came to the patio doors. Minda's mother had a half-filled wine glass in one hand. She supported herself with the other against the rim of the door. "I didn't realize you'd invited friends."

Mrs. Hannaford slurred her words together as though it took too much effort to pronounce them separately. Lexi noticed a glassiness about the older woman's eyes and her unsteady hand on the doorjamb. Minda's mother was drunk.

Lexi glanced at Minda. Minda sat with her shoulders hunched, head down.

Mrs. Hannaford tottered a bit on the threshold of the door. Lexi was afraid she might fall. But the woman righted herself and announced, "My glass is getting empty. You'll have to excuse me." And she faded silently into the house. Todd and Lexi stared at each other across Minda's bent posture. Lexi was the first to speak.

"I'm sorry if we came at at bad time." She glanced at Todd. "Maybe Todd and I should just pretend we didn't come here today."

It was no wonder Minda was lashing out at people. If Lexi's mother were ever like that . . . She shuddered.

"Give us the dress and we'll go," Todd said softly. "Then you can go and talk to your mom."

"My mother and I don't talk," Minda said bitterly as she stood up. "I'll go get the dress." She was so subdued when she carried the wide, frilly gown onto the patio that Lexi hardly recognized her.

"Here, take the dumb dress." She thrust it roughly toward Lexi.

Lexi embraced the frilled layers and murmured, "Thanks."

Minda only stared at her.

Todd, who had been studying the dress, looked up. "Looks like the dress came through the kidnapping without a scratch. Maybe we'd better get it back to the set. This production is set to go off in only a few hours."

Lexi nodded. "See you there, Minda?"

The girl was silent, lost in her own thoughts. Todd and Lexi slipped away.

The return trip was a quiet one. Finally, Todd broke the silence.

"I was really proud of you today."

"Of me? Why?"

"You had every right to read Minda the riot act—but you didn't."

"Did you see her mother? How could I say anything to her when—"

"You're pretty special, that's all I can say." Todd turned to smile at her. His eyes were soft and dark, like Lexi imagined the ocean to be at dusk. Her heart suddenly seemed stuck in her throat.

"Todd, I wanted to tell you . . ." Suddenly it seemed very important that Lexi tell Todd about Ben. They would no doubt meet tonight at the production. She didn't want Todd to be shocked or surprised.

But before the words came, Todd exclaimed, "What's going on here?"

Several cast members had the antebellum plantation backdrop outside. One boy was waving frantically at Lexi and Todd.

He yelled into the car as they pulled up, "Somebody tripped and fell into this backdrop! Can you help us get it repaired, Todd? Mrs. Waverly is having a coronary on the stage!"

Todd flipped off the ignition and jumped from the car. "Can you get home with the dress, Lexi? Looks like I'm needed here."

She nodded. All she could hope for now was a few minutes before the production to explain about Ben.

When she reached home, things were just as exciting there.

Ben came to the door clapping his hands and chanting, "Flowers! Flowers! Flowers!"

Lexi hung her dress in the front hall, rumpled his hair distractedly and went to look for the flowers.

Her mother was watering them—twelve long-stemmed red roses in a crystal florist's vase. A card on a long plastic prong jutted from the greens and baby's breath in which the roses were nestled.

Lexi took the tiny card with shaking hands.

For the best singing partner I've ever had. Todd.

"They're beautiful!" Lexi gasped, running a finger over the velvet petal of a rose.

"And there's more," Marilyn rejoined. "I think

this boy must like you very much." She handed Lexi a white florist's box.

With shaking fingers, Lexi tore into the ribbon-wrapped box. Inside was a corsage of delicate tea roses and tiny blue carnation pom poms. On the second card in Todd's bold scrawl were the words: *And something for you to wear on stage tonight—Todd.*

"Oh . . ." Lexi breathed, speechless.

Her mother was less taken up with the moment. Practical as usual, Mrs. Leighton asked, "Not meaning to sound mercenary, but where does this boy earn his money? He's invested quite a sum in these flowers."

"Oh, Mother!" Lexi retorted; then she added, "He works for his brother who owns a garage. He also has a second job."

"Sounds like an ambitious boy. What's the second job?"

"I don't know, really. He is very quiet about it. He works for his mother, though. She's an administrator for some local or government program. She has an office uptown. That's all I know."

"I'm anxious to meet this young man. I'm surprised you haven't brought him home before this."

Lexi turned her face away from her mother guiltily. Her mother would be terribly hurt to learn that Lexi had not encouraged Todd to come here because of Ben, but Lexi was having difficulty sorting her own emotions in that area. Jerry Randall was just a memory in her life now, and she didn't want Todd to become the same.

Ben meandered into the living room. He'd been foraging in the flowerbed. In his hands were a ragged assortment of dandelions, petunias and daisies, along with a smattering of grass clippings. The smile he wore nearly split his face in two.

"Flowers for Lexi! Flowers for Lexi!" he chanted. Proudly, he presented his sister with his own floral offering.

Lexi buried her nose in the soft silk of Ben's hair and a new resolve spread over her. So what if Todd Winston didn't like Ben? That was just too bad for Todd! He'd never know what he'd missed. Tonight she'd introduce Ben and Todd. She was *proud* of her brother. In the midst of her own problems, she'd nearly forgotten that fact. It was high time she remembered what was important.

"Lexi crying?" Ben stuck an inquiring finger in Lexi's ear.

"No, Ben. This time Lexi's laughing." She squeezed his soft round cheeks between her palms. "Tonight I've got a friend I want you to meet."

"Friend, friend, friend," Ben repeated happily.

"That's right, Ben. And tonight I'll find out just how *good* a friend he is . . ."

The musical was a rip-roaring, all-out success. The summer band sailed through the overture and finale flawlessly but for an occasional missed note from a contrary French horn. Minda sat straight and pale in her chair.

Jennifer had filled in at the last moment for a soloist stricken with food poisoning, and she was beaming from ear to ear at the praise her last-minute contribution had generated.

But best of all had been Todd and Lexi's duet. The

tattered antebellum backdrop had become enchanted. Lexi, with the fragrance of her corsage teasing her nostrils and the feel of Todd's hand placed tenderly at her waist, had sung like she'd never sung before. When the curtain came down, he'd spun her around with a rib-crushing hug.

Lexi could still feel the tickly excitement she'd felt in her midsection. Whatever happened next, whatever happened between Todd and Ben, she would always remember this moment with pleasure.

"Am I going to get to meet your parents tonight, Lexi?" Todd whispered in her ear. "The crowd is thinning out. Are they here?"

"Uh huh," Lexi nodded, straining to catch a glimpse of them. "Are yours?"

"You bet. My mom said she wouldn't miss this for anything—meeting you, I mean. She said she wants to meet the girl for whom I'd buy roses. She didn't think there was anyone important enough to part me from my hard-earned money." He grinned teasingly.

"They're wonderful flowers, Todd. My first roses."

"Good. That way you'll always remember whom they came from."

"How could I ever forget?" Lexi turned to smile at him. She felt warm and happy, cold and nervous, all at once. From the corner of her eye, she could see her parents and Ben making their way to the front of the auditorium.

It was too late now. She no longer had time to tell Todd that she had a retarded brother. It was up to Ben and Todd now. Lexi steeled herself, her mind reeling. Could Ben charm Todd with his loving ways? Would Todd allow him to?

She bent over and opened her arms to Ben as he broke away from his parents and came toward her. But Ben's eyes weren't focused on Lexi.

Screeching "Big fellow! Big fellow! Best friend!" Ben shot past Lexi and into Todd's open arms.

Chapter Eight

"Best friend, best friend," Ben crooned, joyfully stroking his hands across Todd's cheeks.

Laughing, Todd secured his grip on the little boy. "Hi, Ben. Did you come to see me sing?"

"Best friend sing, Lexi sing." Ben pointed at his dumbfounded sister.

With a conscious effort, Lexi managed to shut her gaping jaw.

"Do you know Lexi, Ben?" Todd asked, obviously surprised. Then understanding began to dance across his features. "Leighton! Ben Leighton, Lexi Leighton! But . . ." Todd obviously was puzzling out an answer. "Ben, are your mom and dad's names Beverly and John Leighton?"

"Ben's parents names are Jim and Marilyn. Hello, Todd," Jim Leighton spoke as he extended a hand in greeting. "I see you almost every morning at Camp Courage, but I've never had time to introduce myself. I know there's another Leighton family in town, but we've never met. Lexi is the only one in our family who seems to be getting out and meeting people."

Todd's eyes widened in confusion as he stared at Lexi. "Then you and Ben are—"

"Sister and brother," she finished for him. Things seemed to be happening too quickly for either of them. Then Todd's parents descended on the little group.

Mrs. Winston, a trim, businesslike woman in a dark suit, spoke first. "Beautiful duet, you two! I was so proud—" Then she leaned over to see Ben pulling at her sleeve from his perch in Todd's arms.

"Well, hello, Ben! How are you today?"

Did everyone in town know Ben? Lexi's head spun back and forth between Todd and his mother. What was happening here, anyway? Before she could ask, Mrs. Winston began to introduce herself to Lexi's parents.

"I'm Renee Winston. I'm the coordinator for all handicapped learning programs within the county. I believe you spoke with my assistant about Ben. Your son and mine have become close friends this summer. We enjoy Ben in our program. He's like a ray of sunshine. Isn't he, Todd?"

Todd released the grip his gaze had on Lexi to turn to his mother. "You bet. Isn't that right, little fellow?"

"Little fellow." Ben pointed to himself. "Big fellow," and he turned his pointing finger on Todd.

"Ben loves day camp," Mrs. Leighton enthused, "and he's crazy about Little League."

"Todd is his coach," Mrs. Winston informed her, smiling broadly at her son. "Last year he had a team of little girls, but we had to put an end to that. We had sixteen broken hearts at the end of the year when he couldn't take them all to the closing banquet."

"I can see why," Mrs. Leighton grinned. Lexi wanted to sink into the floor when her mother did things like that, but for the moment she let it pass. There was too much happening for her to comprehend it all.

"Todd and I take a group of the children camping once a month all summer long," Renee continued. "Consider letting Ben come with us sometime. We'll take very good care of him."

The mystery of the camping trip was solved! Lexi shook her head in amazement.

"Let's all go out and celebrate," Todd's father suggested, breaking into Lexi's daze. The tall, striking man had been silent until now. "The kids sang a wonderful duet, and it seems that young Ben has made us all mutual friends. Anyone for ice cream?" They all nodded—especially Ben.

"Maybe I should get out of this dress first," Lexi ventured. She'd almost forgotten the wide skirt with its metal hoops.

"And I'll escape from this tux." Todd ran a finger around the rim of his collar. "We'll meet you at the Ice Cream Factory in half an hour. Don't eat it all before we get there."

Ben tugged on his parents' hands, eager to be on his way. Lexi and Todd parted silently, going to their separate dressing rooms to change.

It was not until they were reunited in Todd's '49 Ford that Todd spoke.

"Why didn't you tell me about Ben, Lexi?"

She could hear the anger in his voice. And the disappointment.

"I—I was afraid, Todd."

"Afraid to tell me about a good kid like Ben? Don't you know what a great little brother you have?"

Lexi wanted to close her eyes and cover her ears against his anger, but she knew she deserved it.

Todd began to unleash some of his frustration. "Lexi, there's nothing wrong with having a retarded child in your family! That's nothing to be ashamed of. I've been working for my mom at Camp Courage since I was thirteen and I've never seen any braver, stronger or more loving people anywhere else! And . . ." Todd's tone was hurt. "Why didn't you trust me, Lexi? You should have known it wouldn't matter to me whether you had a retarded brother or not."

"Todd . . ." Lexi traced a pattern across his face with her hand, much as Ben had done. Tears streamed down her cheeks in rivulets. "It wasn't because I'm ashamed of Ben. I'm proud of him. He's already achieved more than any of us ever dreamed he could. But not everyone understands, Todd. When Jerry didn't, I thought—"

"Jerry? Jerry Randall? What does he have to do with this?"

"When we moved here Jerry Randall asked me out—you remember. The next day he came over to my house. When he saw Ben, Jerry got all flustered and left. He never called again, Todd. He seemed frightened to be around my brother."

"So that's why I overheard Jerry tell you that you

already had strikes against you! He meant Ben!" Todd mused, more to himself than to Lexi.

She nodded. "I should have known better, but I thought that it might be best not to mention Ben at first. You know, until people got to know me. Then when Minda—"

"Minda's involved in *this* too?"

"She came to see me. Ben was on the gate. She called him a retard and said that people like him shouldn't be allowed out in public. I suppose she was so miserable inside because of her parents that she didn't care what she said or whom she hurt, but it just reinforced my idea not to mention Ben. I'm not ashamed of Ben, Todd. I just don't want him to be hurt!"

It was as though the tight little walls she'd constructed inside herself all crumbled at once. Every hurt and emotion and question she'd held inside came tumbling out on a wash of tears.

"I don't know why all this happened to us, Todd. Since we moved to Cedar River, it's been like a curse to have a retarded brother. Why did God pick my family? Why us? Why Ben?"

Todd's eyes were wide and dark. When he finally spoke, his words shocked Lexi from her tears. "Who says God did this to you? Who say's God made Ben the way he is?"

"But—"

"You sound just like an insurance form, Lexi!"

"What?"

"You know, 'We insure everything except in case of an "act of God."' That makes my dad really mad. He says that people are always assuming that God sits up on some big throne in heaven deciding who's going to be punished next, sending wars and famines and punishment down from the clouds. He thinks people have it all backward and I agree with him."

"What do you mean?" Lexi asked.

"I don't think God intentionally sends bad things to happen to people—sickness or injury—or handicapped children. He would be awfully hard to love if that's the kind of God He was. I'd rather think that He's there to *help* us when bad things happen, not to cause them."

"That's sort of what Mrs. Waverly told me once," Lexi murmured to herself.

Todd smiled. "Yeah, I know. We talked about this a lot last year in the high school Sunday school class. Mrs. Waverly was our teacher. She made us memorize a verse from Psalms." He leaned back in the seat for a moment and then began to quote: " 'I lift mine eyes to the hills; from where does my help come? My help comes from the Lord, Maker of heaven and earth.' "

" 'My *help* comes from the Lord . . . ' "

" . . . not my *trouble*."

"You mean I've had it all backward?"

"I don't know. Have you?"

Lexi sighed. "I think so. Everything turned upside down when we had to move. I lost all my friends, my home—"

"But you have a new home and," his eyes brightened, "new friends."

"I'm beginning to realize that."

Todd was quiet for a long time. Finally, when he

looked at Lexi, his blue eyes were warm with compassion.

"I'm sorry if I sounded angry with you. I had no idea about what had happened with Jerry or Minda." He ran sturdy fingers through his sun-bleached hair. "I just get so angry with people who have these warped notions about the retarded. They don't seem to think the handicapped have feelings, or emotions, or a capacity to love. That's why I like coaching the Little League teams at Camp Courage. No one out there ever tells a child he can't do something, that he's not smart enough. If no one tells them that, the handicapped won't think that way. And they achieve some pretty remarkable things."

"Like Ben's mural."

"Hey! I saw that out at the camp! Sorry I didn't recognize you—it would have saved us a lot of time and trouble." Todd grinned widely. "But I never think of you as having purple hair!"

Lexi punched him in the arm. She was nearly dizzy with relief and joy. "Well, you were quite a mystery around our house yourself. I'd always been Ben's best friend until you came along. That was pretty hard on my ego, you know. I've got to teach Ben to remember names. If he had known your name, we wouldn't have had any secrets from each other." Then she turned an accusing finger Todd's way. "You didn't exactly announce what your job for your mother was, you know."

"I know it. It's hard to explain to people why I love it. Sometimes it's just easier to keep my mouth shut."

"You've just described *my* feelings, Todd."

"I'm glad we got that settled." Todd stretched in his seat. "We'd better get going before Ben and his buddies eat all the ice cream."

Lexi lay her head back against the high seat as Todd drove to meet their parents. All the questions she'd carried were erased and she was eager to give that little brother of hers a hug. He'd helped to tie her and Todd together in a way more special and more wonderful than she'd ever dreamed. Now they both had Ben to love.

Things were finally working out. Jennifer and Peggy had become Lexi's good friends. Though she and Minda hadn't come to terms with each other, she wasn't ready to give up on her quite yet. Lexi smiled to herself. Maybe life *would* be good here in Cedar River.

Can Lexi and Minda resolve their differences, or will Minda's family problems engulf them both? Find out in Cedar River Daydreams 2, *Trouble with a Capital "T."*

A Note From Judy

I'm glad you're reading *Cedar River Daydreams*! I hope I've given you something to think about as well as a story to entertain you. If you feel you have any of the problems that Lexi and her friends experience, I encourage you to talk with your parents, a pastor, or a trusted adult friend. There are many people who care about you!

Also, I enjoy hearing from my readers, so if you'd like to write, my address is:

Judy Baer
Bethany House Publishers
6820 Auto Club Road
Minneapolis, MN 55438

Please include an addressed, stamped envelope if you would like an answer. Thanks.